He had gone away and never looked back

Lacey was going home, to the only house in town where Martin wouldn't get over the threshold.

"You can't come in," she warned at the gate.

"I know that."

"Then go away." She dragged the gate shut and spoke through the bars. "I never wanted you to come back. I had a feeling you'd cause trouble. Well, you're causing none for me. So good night, and I'd very much like it to be goodbye."

"I don't believe you," said Martin, eyes hard, mouth unsmiling. She wanted to scream. She hated him. He was so sure of himself that he could believe that five years later she was still there for the taking.

"I'm going to marry Paul," she reminded herself in a whisper, *and then I'll be safe.*

Books by Jane Donnelly

HARLEQUIN ROMANCES

These books may be available at your local bookseller.

For a list of all titles currently available,
send your name and address to:

Harlequin Reader Service
P.O. Box 52040, Phoenix, AZ 85072-2040
Canadian address: P.O. Box 2800, Postal Station A,
5170 Yonge St., Willowdale, Ont. M2N 5T5

A Fierce Encounter

Jane Donnelly

Harlequin Books

TORONTO • NEW YORK • LONDON
AMSTERDAM • PARIS • SYDNEY • HAMBURG
STOCKHOLM • ATHENS • TOKYO • MILAN

Original hardcover edition published in 1983
by Mills & Boon Limited

ISBN 0-373-02635-8

Harlequin Romance first edition August 1984

Printed in U.S.A.

CHAPTER ONE

'WHAT about Martin Jackson?' said somebody. 'He came from round here and he's a celebrity, and he might even get us on TV if we asked him to open the festival.'

Over my dead body, thought Lacey Allen, surprising herself by the violence of her response to that suggestion, because at this stage it was only talk, and she hadn't set eyes on the man in the flesh for nearly five years.

It was a cold November day, with sleet on the tall narrow pointed windows, and making the roads outside slippery and treacherous. The vast room was chilly. The oil heaters set around only warmed it in spots, most of the heat rose up to the beams of the high ceiling and filtered out into the sky.

Once this had been a magistrates' court over the old jail, now it was an arts and crafts market, but the summer season was long gone and the Christmas trade was off to a slow start. Of the two men and four women who were up here not one was a customer. They were all hanging around their stalls, waiting for somebody to come in or something to happen, and drinking coffee.

Lacey sat warming her fingers round her red enamel mug, huddled in a blue quilted jacket. She had smoky-blue eyes, fairish hair that looked tousled unless she brushed it a lot. She was prettier than she knew, especially when she smiled; but most of the time she was a serious-minded girl who looked serious. The walls of her corner were covered with small neatly framed watercolours of local scenes, that sold quite well when holidaymakers were around.

This morning it seemed a waste of time sitting here, and Lacey was bored. A winter break would have been good, a few days in the sun somewhere, but her father needed her around. She wasn't a dedicated artist, but he was, and he was her real job.

Porteus Phipps, a potter, was reading a newspaper on the next stand to hers, rustling the pages, and a radio was tuned to a D.J. playing pop. For the moment no one was talking, although they were usually a chatty crowd. Lacey had a husky voice, unusual and attractive. Into the silence she said, 'There used to be a hiring mop here in Chadsford, the last Saturday of July. Anyone who fancied a change of job or was looking for work could put themselves up for hire for twelve months.'

'There's fascinating,' said Porteus, a portly pleasant bearded man. 'The things you learn having a librarian for a lover!'

Paul Behague, Lacey's steady, was a freelance journalist as well as being in charge of the local library. Last night he had read her his last article for the *Chadsford Mercury*, all about the hiring fairs that had flourished here from medieval times until the end of the last century.

'And I've been thinking,' she went on, 'that maybe we're all in the wrong business. Maybe next year we should all put ourselves up for hire.'

That got them smiling, and a bawdy guffaw from Porteus, who wanted to know, 'How much?'

'Depends,' she joked, 'on what you might be expecting for your money. And it need only be for a fortnight, because then there was the runaway mop when anybody who got a raw deal could come back and try again.'

That was how the idea of putting on a festival in the Midland market town of Chadsford came about. At first they were just talking to pass the time, tossing ideas around that made the summer seem closer. Then, suddenly, a serious note crept in. There were local charities desperate for money, and for shops and restaurants and hotels anything that brought in the customers would be a godsend.

Lacey thought that perhaps Martin Jackson wouldn't come. As a television reporter he was a man who could well have that Saturday in July spoken for, even if he was off duty. She was elected on to the festival committee when it was set up, but his name seemed to be almost everybody's first choice, and she had no objections that would have made any sense. She could hardly say, 'He was bad luck to me. If he opens the festival lightning will strike somewhere.'

So a letter was sent, and a letter came back in which Martin Jackson said he would be delighted to open Chadsford's first festival of Art and Industry on July the thirtieth at ten o'clock.

It was stupid, but it did take some of the fun out of things. Lacey had fun, helping the Arts Centre get organised, rehearsing in a melodrama-matineee that would be playing three afternoons each week in the town's little theatre. Paul had written that, it was based loosely on a local Victorian *cause célèbre*. All sorts of shows and exhibitions, and an actual hiring mop, were planned. Fairground folk were coming in, all the fun-of-the-fair in a meadow on the outskirts of town. There would be plenty to do and see, and if the festival was a success it could become an annual event.

But for weeks before Lacey was haunted by Martin Jackson's all too familiar face. She never quite got used to seeing the crisply cut dark curly hair, the wide cheekbones, the high-bridged nose with the flaring nostrils, no matter how often she passed the posters. And if a new one appeared it always gave her a slight shock.

She caught herself deliberately looking away, and once she made herself turn back. That was the week before the festival when she went into the next town where one of the shops had a poster in the window. Lacey had let her eyes slide away as though that was the man himself, in the delicatessen, watching her through the glass. She ducked her head and quickened her step. Idiot, she thought, and took the three steps back and stared hard at the poster.

This was a piece of paper, for heaven's sake. If she couldn't face this what was likely to happen on Saturday, if she had to meet him alive and breathing? Nothing was going to happen. He might hardly remember her. It would be odd if he didn't, because for nineteen years they had lived in the same town and disliked each other heartily. But since then his life had been crammed. Big exciting things had happened to him and any memories he had of Lacey Allen would be very small fry.

She shouldn't be worrying. He wouldn't be wasting time on her, and she wouldn't have to meet him because she wasn't part of the welcoming committee like her father was. He'd have to come looking for her, and she knew for certain that he would not be doing that.

Lacey's father had been a leading light in organising the festival. Lacey and Porteus had gone along to ask his opinion that first morning. He was in his studio in the big Edwardian house on the hill, with a half-finished painting on his easel. He didn't like to be disturbed at work and Lacey always tapped on the studio door before she went in.

She might have waited till evening to find out what he thought about the idea of a festival, but then the others would have asked somebody else about it first; and as well as being the town's leading artist Laurence Allen was also chairman of the council. The obvious man to consult; and he agreed, almost at once, that it could be a viable project.

If he had been against it Lacey might have lost interest. There would have been a festival because others were enthusiastic, but Lacey had always set great store on her father's opinion. Her father was something special, a tall handsome man with a thatch of silver hair, and both charm and talent. Lacey was proud of him. Her mother had died when she was too young to remember, and Aunt Helena, her father's sister, had reared Laccy to appreciate the privilege of being Laurence Allen's daughter.

He hadn't been too pleased at the choice of Martin Jackson to open the festival, but he had agreed that a television face and name might attract the fans. People would come to see, so Laurence Allen had smiled his charming lopsided smile, and shrugged, and accepted the proposal to write and invite Jackson.

Later, at home, he had admitted to Lacey that he thought a better choice could have been made. He had expected his own name to have been put forward, but he said nothing about that, only that he had always considered Martin Jackson 'a very brash young man.'

Lacey agreed fervently. 'But he might have improved,' she said. 'Anyhow, he won't bother us. He'll just make a little speech and declare the festival open, won't he? He isn't likely to hang around for long—I shouldn't think life in Chadsford is exciting enough for him these days.'

'If I'm any judge,' her father had said, relaxing in the high-backed leather armchair, near the open fire in the marble fireplace in the drawing room, 'he'll ask a fee that will make them think again.'

As it happened he didn't ask any fee at all, and Lacey supposed that was decent of him. Although he must be earning a packet, so why shouldn't he support a little charity from time to time?

She was teased. There were plenty of folk around who remembered how it had been between herself and Martin. She was three years younger than he was, in the same town, with the same friends, for a little while at the same school, and she had hated him. Well no, not hate. She had never actually hated anyone. But every time they met there was a clash of personalities. He needled her, deliberately and devilishly, so that she would cross the street any day to avoid him. In her teens she had looked on him as a jinx. When his shadow fell across her it was going to be a bad day.

In those days he seemed to find everything funny, especially her. She had been a serious child on the whole, working hard, doing her best, and he was clever, the smartest, the one who could do anything he put his mind to. Everything came easy for him, and she resented that because life wasn't easy.

'I see your old friend's opening the festival,' old friends said to her, grinning, and Lacey would smile back,

'Oh, that was a long time ago.' They usually went on about how well Martin Jackson had done and she would say, 'Hasn't he? But then everybody expected him to, didn't they? Clever as a wagon-load of monkeys, was our Martin.'

Paul had never met Martin. Paul had come to live and work here only two years ago and he met Lacey on his first morning. She had gone into the town library to collect a book that had been ordered for her father, and Paul Behague had told her how much he admired Laurence Allen's work.

A painting of 'Chadsford from the West Hills' hung in the library, and they stood in front of it, the artist's daughter, and the tall young man in horn-rimmed spectacles with the aquiline features, and Paul said he considered it was a masterpiece.

So did Lacey. She issued the invitation, 'You must come up and meet him,' because Paul Behague was a newcomer and her father liked meeting people who admired him, but she was taken aback by the promptness of his acceptance.

'I'd love to,' said Paul. 'Tonight?'

Some of the gleam in his eyes was probably for her. It was clear that he thought her attractive and, so far as she could judge on this brief first meeting, he seemed pleasing enough himself. 'Yes,' she said, 'I should think tonight will be fine. Make it around eight.'

Her father had taken to Paul at once. He didn't take to everybody and he didn't like strangers being sprung on him, so Lacey served up a particularly good dinner before she told him about this morning. 'I got your book from the library and I met the new man there, and he was so impressed when he realised who I was, I mean who you are, that I invited him to come and meet you, and he said was tonight all right.'

The evening had gone well. Laurence Allen had been in good form and Paul Behague had hung on his words. Lacey was used to that. Her father was usually the centre of attention. She poured drinks, produced coffee and sandwiches, and sat listening to both of them as Paul answered the older man's questions.

During the evening she learned that Paul Behague was alone in town, in a flat in one of the houses overlooking the square. His parents and a sister lived in Eastbourne. He wasn't married, never had been, and this job was a promotion for him. In his last post he had been an assistant librarian in Birmingham. Also he wrote—articles for newspapers and magazines, and one short story broadcast. As he said goodnight to her at her front door he asked Lacey for a date, and she thought she might like that.

'A finely boned face,' her father said, when she went back into the drawing room. 'You can learn a great deal about character from the bones of the face.'

'Yes,' said Lacey, who had heard that before. 'He asked me to have dinner with him on Wednesday.'

Her father looked surprised, although Lacey had eaten plenty of meals with plenty of young men. She had never been short of admirers. Then he smiled.

She enjoyed her evening with Paul. She had liked him from the first, and she still did. There was no other man in her life now, and why should there be when she and Paul suited each other so well?

Paul had heard about Lacey's long-ago vendetta with Martin Jackson and been amused. 'I was talking to Bart Keddy this morning,' he said. 'He was telling me that you and Martin Jackson used to swing punches at each other when you were kids.'

'Get away with you,' Lacey protested. 'Can you imagine me punching anybody? And he's older and bigger than I am. But it's a fact that we never got on.'

'You never mentioned him before,' said Paul, and she asked, quite reasonably,

'Why should I? He'd gone before you came. He was a local lad who got a rise out of riling me, but it was a long time ago and I'm sure he's forgotten all about it. I had.'

Paul had chuckled, 'Bart said all the girls fell for him but you. He's a striking-looking chap.'

Both as boy and man it was a face that stood out in a crowd. Her father had never declared that Martin had a finely boned face, but he had, a bone structure that made him look like an Aztec chief. Except that the mockery was never far below the surface and Aztec chiefs hadn't had much to laugh at.

'But you never fancied him?' said Paul, and she snapped, 'Not if he was the last man in the world.' And a picture flashed into her mind, of darkness and storm like the end of the world and a wild strange terrible night, and she shut it away because it had never happened, it was just a nightmare thought. 'How's the play going?' she asked.

Paul was only starting to write his melodrama then. Now they had had a final dress rehearsal, and on Monday afternoon they would give the first public performance of 'The Tale of Sweet Alice, or Murder Under the Blasted Oak.'

By Friday night everything was ready. The exhibitions included a special showing of Laurence Allen's paintings in the art gallery; and local crafts—tapestry, pottery, woodcarving, jewellery—were being produced in workrooms that were once offices and cells of the old jail, and offered for sale on stalls in the magistrates' court and outside in the tiny exercise yard. There was nothing to do now but pray for fine weather and Lacey should have been relaxing.

Martin *was* comiing. There had always been a faint hope that something would happen to keep him away, but at this stage that was most unlikely, and she knew she would only feel really safe when tomorrow was over and he was gone. Not that he was any threat to her. What could he do except smile and say, 'Hello, are you still here?' Something like that.

Paul had come in for coffee. He had been helping her and the others at the Centre until nearly nine o'clock, and he and Lacey had drunk their coffee in the kitchen because her father and one of his old friends were sitting over brandy and cigars in the drawing room. At half past nine she yawned and Paul said, 'You're right, it's going to be a big day tomorrow.' He drained his coffee and stood up and she almost said, 'Don't go just yet,' but then she stood up too and walked with him to the door and out to his car.

A cloud drifted over the moon as Paul said, 'Well, the weather forecast was good,' and Lacey looked up and thought, I could give that cloud a name.

'It's going to be fun,' she said. 'It feels like before a party.'

'When everything's ready and waiting and you're hoping the guests will turn up.' There were often parties in this house, small dinner parties usually with her father at the head of the table, but Lacey entertained too, planning ahead so that everything went smoothly. The guests always came and nothing very surprising ever happened. She smiled, 'That's it. Roll on tomorrow!' And keep one guest well away from me, she thought.

Paul kissed her tenderly and she clung to him, kissing back with an ardour that stirred him so that he wished he had kissed her in the house rather than out here. One day they would marry. Everybody who knew them knew that, but he wished she was coming home with him now. Lacey drew away and said, 'Go careful on the corners. See you for lunch.'

She watched the car take the first corner and stood where she was for a few moments longer, wondering if her reluctance to move out of Paul's arms had been passion or panic. She would have liked him with her tomorrow. She could have done with him by her side and his ring on her finger.

She wore rings, silver in various patterns, designed and made by one of the girls in the Arts Centre. The thickest was on the third finger of her right hand, and she swopped it with the rings on the same finger of her left. She was as good as engaged. All she had to do was name a day. Paul had told her that often enough in the last twelve months. So had his sister, with whom Lacey got on very well. 'Why don't you make an honest man of my brother?' Jenny, married herself with two children, had asked the last time Lacey went down to spend a weekend with his parents.

Lacey was happy too. Happy and lucky. But tonight she was restless with a nervous tension that could keep her awake half the night, and it wasn't late enough to go to bed. Her father and his guest could be chatting for hours yet, so that ruled out curling up in front of the television. She'd finished the book she was reading and hadn't had the time to get another, and it was a nice night for a walk and there was somebody who was always ready to walk with Lacey.

A. Bowden's wool shop was in one of the side streets, and as long as Lacey could remember Mrs Bowden had lived there alone. Mr Bowden hadn't come back from D-

Day, but all that was before Lacey was born. The Mrs Bowden she knew had always seemed fat, jolly and middle-aged. For the past three years Lacey had been walking her dog, and now she went down the little entry to the back of the house. The lights were still on in Mrs Bowden's sitting room and the kitchen, and Lacey gave her signal knock—one tap, two quick, a pause and then three slow—and got a baying like a joyful Hound of the Baskervilles in response.

Mrs Bowden looked out, all smiles, and a huge hairy dog, pale beige in colour, hurled itself at Lacey who braced herself against the wall of the house when the paws descended on her shoulders. Peering round the shaggy head, she asked, 'Is it all right if I walk him round town? Then I could take him home with me and bring him back tomorrow night.'

'He'd like that,' said Mrs Bowden, 'But don't let him be telling you he's had no supper.'

The dog padded along beside her; a well trained animal, he kept to heel in the streets, but at the end of the road he stopped, head on one side, sniffing the slight breeze. The way he loved led up to the common, and Lacey said, 'You know, I was thinking the same thing.' It was late to go walking over the hills, but it was a light night, and Jet was a big dog, and that was where she wanted to go.

She wasn't walking aimlessly. She set off in a definite direction and the dog raced ahead of her, bounding over the grass and bracken. She hadn't been this way for a long time, but the moors and the woods only changed for the seasons, and for natural growth and decay. It was high summer now, the ground was soft, leaves were on the trees, and after a while Lacey reached a clearing in a hollow where there had been a building, a hut. It was still recognisable. Just. There were walls and a gap where the door had hung, but the roof had gone and the walls had crumbled and grass and lichen grew over and around.

She stood very still, listening to the hooting of an owl and the sighing of the trees, and Jet crashing around in the undergrowth. A twig snapped, under the great paws, but it startled her as though somebody was stalking her, and she turned hurriedly away. It had to be getting on for eleven by now. Coming out here alone at this time was worse than foolhardy. If she'd had to come why not by daylight. Why at all? She hadn't given the place a thought in years and then tonight suddenly, she had had to return and look at it again. What kind of ghosts was she expecting to find waiting for her?

She began to scramble back up the hill, Jet loping easily beside her, and then made herself slow down, although now the night and the moors seemed full of danger and potential violence and her heart was thudding in her chest like a steam engine. Paul would think she had gone out of her mind if she told him, 'After we said goodnight I went for a few miles over the hills and through the woods. Got back home around midnight.'

She hoped she would get back home without meeting a maniac or a mugger, or breaking her leg in a rabbit hole. She prayed as she went, as fast as she dared, and when they got off the common, back to the streets and the lights, her legs were rubbery, and she clutched the thick coarse fur on the dog's back, and his tail swished and he grinned at her. He had had a grand time. This beat trotting round the town any night. 'Just don't you ever tell a soul where we went,' Lacey panted, and walked him sedately the rest of the way home.

The dog slept in the garage when Lacey kept him overnight. He had a bed in there and it was warm, even in winter. If he had been smaller she might have risked smuggling him up to her room. Both her aunt and her father disliked dogs with an abiding antipathy. Laurence Allen had been bitten by one as a child. His sister Helena told the story to Lacey in gory detail when Lacey asked for a dog for her seventh birthday. No animal crossed the threshold of the Allen home—they weren't keen on cats either—but Lacey adored them, and Jet spent almost as much time with her as he did with his owner.

When Aunt Helena was alive she had run this house, and run it very well, with the help of a daily and Lacey. Helena Allen had looked like her brother, tall and handsome, and silver-haired. She had been several years older than he and she had devoted her life to his genius. She saw him as a genius and was pleased at Lacey's flair for art—which was of course nothing compared to her father's, but got Lacey into art college and producing saleable work afterwards. When Helena Allen died she left her brother as a sacred trust to his daughter, and now Lacey ran the home, and nothing about Laurence Allen's lifestyle had changed. His world still revolved around him. He was still as appallingly self-centred as he had always been.

He liked a full English breakfast while he glanced through the *Telegraph* and *Times* and read his mail. Lacey was a coffee girl, sometimes toast, but she cooked his bacon and eggs, and usually left him at the table when she left for the Arts Centre. Most mornings he spent in his studio, or on various outings. He was involved in local politics, chaired a number of committees, and today he would be prominent among the V.I.P.s when Martin Jackson opened the first Chadsford festival, and at the luncheon laid on in the town hall banqueting room.

He frowned over his newspaper as Lacey set down his breakfast plate and she enquired, 'Are the headlines as horrible as ever?'

'Very depressing.' They always were, but it wasn't what he was reading that was depressing Laurence Allen. It was thinking ahead to ten o'clock when he would have to shake hands with that objectionable young man, and wondering what they could possibly have to say to each other.

Lacey suspected something of the sort. She said, 'It's going to be a lovely day. The sun's shining already. That should get the festival off to a good start.' But her father wasn't cheered and when a dog began to bark he demanded, 'Have you brought that hound here again?'

'Not in the house, and I'm taking him off with me now.'

'Don't let it in here, you know my allergy.'

'I'm going.' She poured him another cup of coffee, and then he did start scanning the news, answering her goodbye absentmindedly.

Lacey fed Jet and he walked with her down town to the Arts Centre, where they entered by a side door. Nine o'clock was the usual opening hour, although the artists who had workrooms here came any time they chose. This morning the shops that were putting on special displays for the festival were opening when the town clock struck ten and Martin Jackson gave the word go, and inside the Centre Lacey's colleagues were taking up their positions.

Jet settled into the corner on a tartan travelling rug she kept for him there. Everybody here knew him. He roamed around, upstairs and downstairs and in the exercise yard, being fed titbits and providing a talking point for customers.

Lacey had set up an easel among her display, with a sketch of one of the side streets of Chadsford. She would colour and bring that to life as the visitors watched. She had a portfolio of local scenes roughed out and she hoped to be completing and selling some of them.

You could hear the church clock chime in here, if you listened carefully and it was quiet. But this morning at ten the bells pealed out with five minutes from *Merrie England*—and that meant that the festival was under way, and the main doors were opened and the folk who had been on the streets began to wander in. There was quite a crowd. It was very satisfactory. The schools had broken up and if the weather held this could go on for the whole fortnight.

Martin Jackson, she heard, had declared the festival open and now was loose on the town. So were a T.V. camera team. Chadsford Festival would have its publicity slot on the regional news tonight. Locals came in to tell them in the Centre what was going on and she was quite prepared for Martin to come up the ornate iron staircase from the ground floor and walk round the stalls. Several of the stallholders had known him when he lived in the town. They would chat like old friends, say it was nice to see him again, although there weren't many weeks when they couldn't have turned on their T.V.s and seen him. Not to mention all those posters that had been stuck up everywhere for months and could now, thank heaven, come down again.

Lacey was putting little dabs of bright colour into a window box on her watercolour when she looked up and saw him, and paralysing shock hit her. He was coming straight towards her, walking with that arrogant animal grace she remembered. She felt like the rabbit with the stoat, hedged into her little corner, Martin's eyes holding her fast and Martin coming for her.

She put down her paints and cleared her throat and as he reached her she said, 'Well, if it isn't Black Jack!' He had always, she thought, looked older than he was. Even as a teenager there had been something about the set of his mouth and the piercing blue of his eyes that was never childlike. Since he went she had seen him on television, although she rarely watched through a programme when he was doing the interviewing or the talking. But now she saw how the last five years had scored deep lines, from nose to mouth, and across his brow. The mockery was still there, but she thought he could pass for ten years older and she exclaimed impulsively, 'My God, you've aged!'

'You haven't.' He was smiling at her now and she

remembered how he used to do that, while his eyes watched, aloof from the smile. 'There's no change in you, not by a hair.'

He touched a tendril that was curling on her forehead, winding it round his finger, and the light tug made her scalp tighten. She sat stiffly, backbone rigid, the nerves in the back of her neck knotting. 'Interesting place you have here,' he said.

'You remember it, of course.' Her voice was perfectly controlled. He leaned forward to examine her work on the easel, avoiding comment except for a slight quirk of an eyebrow that was not complimentary.

'The old jail? Sure. Although it was a warehouse in my day. Arts Council grant now, is it?'

'No, we're not subsidised.'

'Who owns the place?'

'I do.' Pride of ownership crept into her voice, because this centre was her enterprise and her baby. 'The stalls and workrooms are leased.'

It was a good place for artists to work and sell. Without it times would be harder than they were for all of them, and so far as she was concerned the building was non-profit making. It just broke even on overheads.

None of this concerned him, but it was easier to talk than to stay quiet. 'And you bought a jail?' he said. 'It figures.'

'It went up for sale,' she told him. 'And Aunt Helena had left me a little money. It was going for a song.'

He meant she was a prisoner. After all this time he could still come out with that old jibe. She said coolly, 'I bought an art centre. Do browse around. We have some very talented work.'

He was scanning the walls where her own work hung, and she asked, 'Anywhere in particular you're interested in?'

He moved, skirting Jet, looking up and down the rows of little pictures. 'There used to be an old charcoal burner's hut on the hills. Have you ever painted that?'

'No.' Dear heaven, *no!* People were listening! He was the celebrity, instantly recognisable by the public and backed by the little group of locals who were accompanying him round the festival. Everybody was listening to this.

'Perhaps you could paint it for me from memory,' he said. He turned and his eyes met hers, and her chin lifted, as it always had when her back seemed to be to the wall. And that was only with him. With no one else had she ever felt this clash of temperament. She couldn't believe that it could be as overwhelming as though he had never gone away.

Surely the years should have dulled it to a memory. But it rose in her, sharp and savage, and Lacey said, smiling straight at him, her eyes glinting with a sparkle he would know for anger, 'I can't remember how it was, but it's been just a few bricks for a long time. How about one of your old school? You were always the star there.'

'All right,' he said. 'Put me down for the old school.' The Boys' Grammar School was a mock Gothic building of grey stone with arches around a quadrangle. There wasn't a picture of it up on the wall, but she could soon produce one, and she wouldn't turn down a sale although she knew Martin thought her artistic talent was run-of-the-mill. He was unlikely to hang anything of hers in any home of his, but his cheque would be money in the bank.

'Your dog?' Jet was watching it all, and Martin probably remembered Laurence Allen's allergy, because he asked, 'Does he live in the jail?' as if he knew no dog would live in the house.

'He lives with Mrs Bowden at the wool shop.' Lacey bent across to scratch Jet's chin because she and Jet had an understanding, and dogs were funny creatures and Jet was smart and if he tuned in to the way Lacey was feeling he could be at Martin's throat. She said, 'His name's Jet.'

'Jet?' There wasn't a black hair on him.

'Short for Jetsam. Mrs Bowden found him on the beach at Blackpool and nobody claimed him, so she adopted him. But her house isn't very big.' And Jet was huge. 'He was smaller then,' said Lacey. 'He's grown a lot.'

Martin laughed. 'That's a lot of dog.' He patted the rough beige fur, brushing Lacey's hand, and her fingers stilled and slipped away and she held them tight in her other hand.

Porteus was down in his workroom, throwing pots on a wheel, but Maisie, his girl-friend and fellow potter, was on the pottery stand waiting for Martin to come her way. All of them were. Maisie beamed as he looked over and he looked back at Lacey and said, pleasantly and casually, 'See you.'

That was a cliché, she thought. She hoped. 'How long can you give me for this picture you've ordered?' She picked up her paints again.

'Take all the time you need,' he said, and she was surprised that her hand was steady enough to go on dotting in the little scarlet flowers when inside she was shaking like a leaf.

'You've got to admit he's super,' said Maisie, after Martin had bought something from most of the stalls and gone down the staircase stopping at the top to sign an autograph book but not to look across at Lacey again.

'Super,' said Lacey. She was all right now. She had stopped shaking. Of course, 'See you' meant nothing more than goodbye, and the painting of his old school could be posted on to him. That feeling of regression had been brief, and now it was over and she had nothing further to worry about. After the official lunch he would be into his car and away, and the festival was heading for success, if this morning was anything to go by.

She could have sketched the Grammar School from

memory, and if anyone else had given her a commission she would have started on it right away. But this morning she went on colouring in the roughed out sketches, and sold a couple more pictures and left a friend keeping an eye on her display when she took Jet off with her to have lunch with Paul.

Their favourite eating place for lunch was the Mulberry Tree, a pub in the middle of town. Visitors were crowding into it today, but Lacey and Paul carried out glasses of lager, two ploughman's, and a steak and kidney pie for Jet, into the gardens at the back, which were dominated by the giant mulberry tree, with thick clusters of juicy dark red berries among the green leaves. There they sat on the grass, the tray between them and Jet sprawled at Lacey's feet, and discussed the festival so far.

There was a display of old papers and photographs of Chadsford set out in the library and all morning the public had been trooping through. Paul was pleased about that, and Lacey was pleased at the numbers who had come to look and buy at the Arts Centre. The sun was blazing down. There was music in the air and a general holiday spirit.

Peter had seen the opening ceremony, which took place on the town hall steps next to the library, and told her all about it, including Martin Jackson's speech. Martin had talked about the time when he had lived here. He had mentioned several people by name with affection, and gratitude in some cases. Friends, teachers, neighbours. He had described her father who was standing beside him as one of our greatest living artists, an inspiration to everybody who knew him, and seemed to single him out when he was thanking the committee for asking him back home, as it were. Then he had wished the festival all the luck in the world, and declared it open.

Lacey took a sip of her iced lager. 'Very nice touch,' she said grimly, because Martin had never appreciated her father's work. The bit about 'one of the greatest living artists' would certainly be tongue-in-cheek, and she bet he guessed that if anybody was against inviting him here as guest of honour it would be Laurence Allen. Martin remembered old times all right. He was still getting in the last laugh.

She began to feed Jet with her cheese, he had soon demolished his pie and was now eyeing her plate and drooling. Then she gave him half her hunk of new bread, and asked, 'What shall I cook for your dinner tomorrow?'

'Surprise me,' said Paul.

'You got the bid in, of course?'

'Of course.'

Another gimmick for the festival was based on the old traditional hiring mop. Locals were offering their practical talents for hire during the two weeks of the festival. Proceeds towards a mini-bus, for the church youth club and Golden Age club. For the last two week lists had been printed in the *Chadsford Herald* with offers—from babysitting to house painting. In Lacey's case she was prepared to cook somebody four meals during the next fourteen days. Bids could be dropped into a collecting box in front of the town hall, and bidders had to live within the town radius.

Lacey expected Paul's bid to be her highest. They had discussed the most generous contribution they could afford towards the mini-bus, and Paul had dropped in his tender with that figure. The box was collected at midday and the scraps of paper were now being scrutinised by the ladies of the Mothers' Union, who were vetting anything that did not look a hundred per cent bona fide and no funny business.

At first this enterprise had almost got itself launched as the Chadsford Slave Auction, but the vicar was having none of that, so it was demurely and correctly billed as the Hiring Mop. At six o'clock those who had put themselves up for hire met their 'employers' on the

Vicarage lawn, as part of the church fête that was being held today to coincide with the start of Festival Fortnight.

They had been told beforehand who was after their services, so that they could refuse if they wished, and they were all happy with the offers, which were going to bring in a good sum for a good cause. Fancy dress was being worn by most of them. Lacey was done up in mob cap and lavender-sprigged cotton dress with long full skirts. The other girls and women were rather like Lacey; and the men were in various styles of Victorian rustic, from shepherds' smocks to shirt-sleeves, crossed braces and cords, clumping around in boots.

Paul's bid was Lacey's best, and although Paul hadn't managed to get along yet he would be coming later, and she stood with the small dwindling crowd of friends as the vicar read out names, of hired and hirer, and hands were solemnly shaken on the bargain and the contribution to the fund was chalked up on a board while everybody clapped.

This was all a bit of lighthearted fun, but as she stood waiting Lacey found herself looking beyond the lawns with the stalls and the sideshows, towards the trees of the rookery that rose high and dark, and thinking how different this was from the real hiring mops. Everybody here knew where they would sleep tonight and where their next meal would come from. Long ago, if nobody hired you, all hopes had gone for twelve months and the winter might be hard and you might have no shoes on your feet. Her thoughts stayed gloomy, which was odd, because she was not given to gloom, musing on how grim it must have been to perhaps know nothing of the man who hired you. It would be a man, women didn't do much hiring in those days. You would just have to go with him and hope for the best, and although there was always the runaway mop fourteen days later suppose you couldn't run away?

'Miss Lacey,' the vicar announced, and Lacey

gathered her wits and stepped forward. 'Now here,' the Reverend Roderick Beale went on archly, 'we have a small problem.'

Problem? When Lacey had arrived, a little breathless at five to six, she had been told that Paul's bid was the highest, and everybody knew that was all right by Lacey, so what could be the problem? 'A late bid,' said the vicar. 'Just handed in.' His wife was beside him, smiling. She must have brought it, and Lacey waited, resisting the urge to ask, 'What the hell are you on about?'

'Double your best offer,' said the vicar, beaming broadly. 'Now the question is, is a late bid—even one as generous as this—allowed? What are the rules.'

Martin was there. She hadn't noticed him before and she was sure she would have noticed him. He must have walked up in the last minute or two, and it had to be his bid. Mr Beale and his wife had come to Chadsford after Martin Jackson left. They knew nothing about old frictions, and anybody who did would conclude that bygones were bygones, and this was a friendly gesture on Martin's part. Maybe it was. Maybe he didn't feel the turmoil that just looking at him stirred in Lacey.

'So,' the vicar was appealing to Lacey and to all of them, 'what do we do?'

She shrugged, and somebody shouted, 'Going to the highest bidder!' and there was clapping and laughter, then Martin stepped forward hand outstretched, and Lacey had to shake his hand. Anything else would have made a howling spectacle of herself. So they wrote up Martin's bid, which was quite a booster, and Lacey stepped off-centre with her hand through Martin's arm.

'How will you have your four meals?' she asked lightly. 'Breakfast, dinner, tea and supper tomorrow? I presume you're not staying the weekend.'

'No rush.' He smiled down at her and her own smile seemed pinned to her face. 'I'm staying the fortnight.'

She wanted to pull her hand away. She would as

soon as they got through this little crowd round the hiring mop charade. They walked towards the edge of the lawns to where the rockery began, and stood apart, looking at the fête spread out in front of them. Then she asked, 'What on earth could be keeping you in Chadsford?'

'Unfinished business.'

Her head jerked round, but his profile was telling nothing. His jawline had always had that hardness. 'What?' It could be none of her business, but it was a natural question, and suddenly he grinned.

'I've got a couple of weeks going spare, and no particular plans. Now I'm here I reckon I might as well stick around.'

She did not want him around. 'You look ridiculous in that hat,' he said. The mob cap had risen up on her unruly hair and she pulled it down, well over her ears.

'I don't think,' she said, 'that I should enjoy cooking for you.'

'Then you should have spoken up, shouldn't you? A bargain's a bargain, and all these witnesses saw us shake hands.' The tone was bantering, 'So, if you don't want to cook, what are you offering?'

She would have said something cool and cutting, if he had given her a moment. But he suddenly gripped her shoulders, taking her off balance so that she lurched against him, then he yanked off the mob cap and as she spluttered outrage he said, still smiling, 'Not to worry. I'm sure that between the two of us we can come up with something we'd both enjoy.'

CHAPTER TWO

LACEY wasn't looking at Martin. Her gaze ranged over the people and the stalls as though she was searching for a familiar face. In fact she was neither searching nor seeing. She was so aware of the man beside her that what was going on in front of her was just a moving blur of colour. 'We'll stick with cooking,' she said. 'Four meals. Space 'em how you like in the next two weeks.' Doesn't sound long, does it? But a lot can happen in two weeks.' His voice was flat. He sounded that way on the screen too, no words wasted, but everybody listened to him. Warning bells rang in her head. He would always have that power to generate excitement, there would always be that buzz about him. He was going to cause some disturbance here, but not for her, and she turned and walked away, around the edge of the lawn.

He walked beside her. 'Where's Jet?' he asked.

'I took him home—not my home, his—before I came here. He's fine in the Arts Centre. He knows his way around, he keeps between the stalls nicely, only out here he might decide to chase a cat or go for the jackpot on the tombola.'

If she went back into the middle of the church fête she might be able to shake Martin off—somebody would soon relieve her of him, but she could do with a minute or two alone first; so she kept to the outskirts of the lawn and her petticoats flapped at her ankles, hampering her. This was the costume she would be wearing in the melodrama-matinee. In the constricted space of a small stage she hadn't noticed it was a shade too long. She would turn up the hems before Monday, she was tripping instead of striding, and she stopped

28

and said wryly, 'If the women who were hired wore skirts like these I shouldn't think they could make it to the runaway mop, even if they did find they'd got a swine of a master.'

Martin grinned, 'But you wouldn't run away, would you? You'd stay at your post.'

'Some of us have to stay,' she said tartly. 'Or the world would be in a mess.'

'Has nobody told you? It is.'

'And you're the man who covers the trouble spots.' She put her hands on her hips and surveyed him with what she hoped looked like amusement. 'You know, I've sometimes wondered if the trouble's there before you arrive or whether you're the one who sparks it.' She was babbling nonsense.

'Have you?'

'What?'

'Wondered about me.'

Not for a long time. Not until she knew he was coming back. 'Why should I?' she said.

'Why indeed?' Suddenly she had to blink against his hard blue stare and this time, turning her head, she made herself see the others, and there was Paul and she cried, 'There's Paul!' with delight and relief.

'Who's Paul?'

She wanted to say, 'Mine,' but that would have sounded too possessive. She said, 'The one I thought I'd be cooking for,' and lifted her skirts clear of the ground and ran to Paul.

He had spotted her. He waved and smiled, but when she reached him he looked disgruntled and wanted to know, 'What's going on? They tell me Martin Jackson doubled my bid.'

'Yes.'

'That's big of him.' Paul wasn't sure how to figure this, but it was making him uneasy. 'Did he recognise you?'

'Of course he recognised me. I haven't changed that

much in five years.' Not by a hair, Martin had said. 'I told you he came into the Centre this morning.'

Over lunch she had said that Martin had walked in and around and said hello to everybody.

'Why did he want you?' queried Paul. 'Didn't I hear you couldn't stand the sight of each other?'

Martin had followed her. Now he reached them. 'Paul wants to know why you want me,' she said, and Martin grinned and drawled,

'Now there's a question!'

Paul hadn't meant that the way it sounded. She was stirring things herself here. Then she went smoothly on, 'To cook all these meals for you when you've never tasted my cooking!'

'Call it a gamble. And I do remember my old man ate at your house from time to time. He never complained.'

Martin's father and Laurence Allen had belonged to the same clubs. Courtney Jackson had died suddenly, of a stroke, during Martin's last year at Cambridge, and astonished everybody by leaving his son only a mortgaged house. 'Aunt Helena did most of the cooking then,' Lacey reminisced. 'May I have my hat?'

Martin was still carrying it. He handed it over. 'You don't wear this often, do you?'

'There's no need to labour the point, you did mention it looked ridiculous,' she snapped, and rammed it back on her head. 'No, I don't wear it often, we're in fancy dress for heaven's sake. This is my costume for the play we're doing three afternoons a week in the Little Theatre. It's based on the story of Alice Gough.' She smiled at Paul. 'And Paul wrote it.'

'Who do you play?' asked Martin.

'Alice.'

'*Sweet Alice*, of course. This I must see.' He had been a local boy, he knew the old barnstorming tale of seduction and murder. They would be playing it for laughs and hisses, not seriously in any way, but all the same she would rather he didn't come to watch. He could make her forget her lines, he could make her dry up.

He had done that once nearly ten years ago. In those days she had belonged to the Church Youth Club. Martin never had. He was both a leader and a loner, but never a joiner, and for the Christmas show they had put on *Pygmalion*. Lacey often got a leading role, she was good. That year she was Eliza and feeling quite pleased with her cockney accent until she spotted Martin Jackson in the audience. He was in the second row, the only one in a sea of happy friendly faces who looked totally unimpressed. Suddenly she felt an awkward amateur, her shrill mock-cockney seemed ridiculous, and for what seemed an age she was struck dumb. Even when the hiss of the prompter got through she stammered and made such a mess of that scene that she didn't get the lead next Christmas although in the following scene she never glanced his way again and the rest of the play was fine.

'Hello,' said a pretty girl with long straight fair hair, wearing a grey velvet track suit with a flight of pink satin balloons floating across her small neat breasts. She was talking to Martin, moving nervously and biting her lip as she smiled, 'Remember me?'

You should, thought Lacey. She always sends you a Christmas card. You could be the reason her marriage is rocky after only a couple of years. Denice Wheeler had such a crush on you in the old days that she followed you about like your shadow. You must remember that.

'Of course I do,' he said. 'How are you?'

'Oh, bearing up.' Denice smiled bravely. 'It's certainly good to see you again. We often talk about you, you know, all the old gang.'

No, we don't, thought Lacey. You turn up on TV and sometimes you write articles and then somebody mentions you sometimes, but we're all busy living our own lives and you have no place here any more. 'Tony

and Beth are on the skittles run.' Denice touched
Martin's arm. 'Do come, Lacey's monopolised you long
enough.' She smiled at Lacey who, suggested,

'How about dinner tomorrow for your first meal?'

'What's this about you bidding for Lacey?' Denice
Wheeler was getting her confidence back now. 'I'll cook
for you for nothing,' she said gaily. 'Will you come and
have dinner with us before you go?'

'Thank you,' said Martin, and to Lacey, 'What time?'

'Sevenish.' She added ironically, 'My father will be
pleased to see you,' and saw the brief almost
imperceptible hardening of his face.

'I should check on that if I were you,' he said quietly.
'I'm staying at the Cross Keys.'

Denice led him away and Paul asked, 'Will your
father mind?'

'He didn't like Martin any more than I did.' She
watched them go, the broad shoulders, the dark unruly
hair, and Denice dancing along beside him, looking up
at him all the time, gesturing as she talked and tossing
back her hair as she laughed. That couldn't start up
again in a fortnight, could it? Lacey wondered, and saw
trouble and unhappiness ahead if it did. She said, 'He
got on all right with Martin's father. They almost went
into business together once, buying an art gallery in
Worcester, but it fell through. They got on fine, but
Martin always irritated my father.'

'What was he like, Jackson's father?' Paul was taking
an interest in Martin Jackson's background, since
Jackson seemed to be taking an interest in Lacey. He
had gone with Denice, but he and Lacey had looked at
each other as though the light chatter was just a cover-
up. Martin Jackson was a powerful personality, and
Lacey seemed different standing beside him, not
overwhelmed or overshadowed, just different from the
girl Paul knew.

'A nice man,' said Lacey. She smiled fleetingly, 'My
Aunt Helena used to say he was one of the few

remaining gentlemen. Martin wasn't like him at all. Martin was always Black Jack.'

'Black Jack!' Paul echoed, and she laughed.

'It was a nickname.' She was the only one who had used it. Nobody else called him anything but Martin. He hadn't cared much for Black Jack, but she had thought it suited him. 'I'll tell you something,' she said. 'Denice nearly had a nervous breakdown over him. My father might not be too thrilled at having him around for Sunday dinner, but Barry Wheeler will blow his top when he hears Denice has invited Martin Jackson home.'

She sounded cynically amused, and Paul was faintly shocked. Lacey was a considerate girl. He would have expected her to be worried for Denice and Barry. He said, 'Poor old Barry. Still, it was a long time ago, wasn't it?'

'Oh, a lifetime,' Lacey murmured.

'And he won't be here for long.'

'He's staying for the festival.' She saw his start of surprise, and she watched Martin and Denice reach the skittles run, and saw how folk gathered around Martin. The hiring mop sideshow was over now, everyone was wandering around the fête again. 'He had some leave due,' she explained. 'If anything really dramatic happens out there I suppose he could be recalled and sent off to cover it. If not he'll settle for Chadsford and two weeks of the quiet life.' Paul said nothing. 'If he doesn't manage to turn this into a trouble spot,' said Lacey. 'I think I'm getting out of this outfit. The elastic's too tight in the hat and I'm getting a headache, and the skirts are tripping me up, then I'm going home.'

She was getting a headache, there was a throbbing in her temples, and Paul asked, 'Can I come with you?'

'Sure. We'll have some tea at home and then go out on the town.' She linked her hand through his arm and they passed the skittles run as Martin sent a ball bowling down and several skittles flying. He looked up, straight at Lacey, and she said, 'Still knocking 'em for six, I see.'

'You too,' he said.

'What did he mean by that?' Paul enquired as they walked on without stopping, and Lacey shrugged.

'I wouldn't know.' He meant Paul, she had always had her admirers, but men had never made the fools of themselves over her that girls had over him, and presumably still did. She saw photographs in the papers of him with a girl hovering, but it was rarely the same girl twice.

'Was it serious, between him and Denice?' Paul asked, and Lacey said, 'For her it was, I don't think it was for him. She used to cry on my shoulder, but I don't think he cried on anybody's.'

Lacey had changed into her costume in one of the bedrooms in the Vicarage. She ran upstairs now and got out of her flapping skirts and petticoats and back into a blue silk shirtwaister dress she had worn during the day, Downstairs in the kitchen they were still making jugs of orangeade and lemonade, and pots of tea for the refreshment tent, although the fête was almost over, and Martin's bid for Lacey had given them something to gossip about. It seemed a generous gesture, a way of contributing to the funds, but Paul—waiting for Lacey in the hall—had been on the receiving end of a few quips.

As she came down the stairs she heard one of the churchwardens, a local farmer, chuckle and say, 'You want to watch out, lad. I wouldn't want him putting in bids for my missus.'

'Evening, Mr Wagstaff,' said Lacey.

Sam Wagstaff went on chuckling, but Paul was frowning and he stayed silent until he and Lacey let themselves out through the little gate that led from the back of the Vicarage gardens into a leafy lane. Then he said, 'I wish I'd got here earlier. I'd have stopped that pantomime.'

'You mean Martin's bid?'

'It's made me look like a loser.'

'*No*,' said Lacey. Paul was a sensitive man, and Mr Wagstaff's little joke had been at Paul's expense just now.

'I don't trust Jackson,' said Paul.

Lacey swung the bag containing her costume. It was raffia woven, they sold them in the Arts Centre. 'You could be right,' she said, 'I don't know that I would.'

'What does he want with you?'

Paul was jealous and that was silly. Lacey smiled at him and swung the bag along the top of the waving grasses that grew high beneath the hedges of the lane. 'Nothing,' she said, 'except perhaps a bit of verbal sparring for old times' sake. Denice looked as though she doesn't intend to let him out of her sight while he stays around, and she isn't the only one. They'll be queueing up to feed him and house him. He's a celebrity, and he had friends here he's kept in touch with. I'm not in his plans, I promise you.'

'Yes,' said Paul, 'well.' Then he smiled, faintly at first, but shaking his head at his own suspicions and asking solicitously, 'How's the headache?'

'It was the hat,' she said. But she still had a small dull ache behind her eyes, that was tension, not because the hat had been too tight. Martin had no plans. He was staying because he had time on his hands, and she had no cause to feel threatened. Nothing was going to happen to her that would change anything. Her life was planned and Paul was a very important part of it, and there was no need for him to worry. 'What if your father doesn't want him coming to dinner tomorrow?' Paul enquired, and Lacey grimaced,

'Then I suppose I phone the Cross Keys and leave a message saying don't come.' She laughed, but that was what Martin was expecting and it would make her into a ninny. The house was her home as well as her father's, and if he couldn't face eating with Martin two days in a row she could take him a tray up to his studio.

She knew, as she made that decision, that it would annoy her father. He was never crossed. This was a small thing, but he would be upset if she began acting out of character.

She left Paul in front of the television, hoping to catch the opening of Chadsford Festival in the regional news, and turned on her small black and white portable while she took a quick shower and changed for the evening. She shot out of the shower when she heard the word Chadsford and there was Martin, making his speech, and she grabbed up a towel in a reflex action as though he could see her, naked and dripping. She began to rub herself dry vigorously and he was only on screen for a minute. Then the camera did another few minutes covering the festival attractions, and she turned off the set and went into her bedroom.

She could still see him. She could see him when she looked into the mirror at her own face. She could see him when she closed her eyes. She took a sleeveless scoop-necked white and scarlet polka-dotted dress out of the wardrobe, and sat down in bra and pants to fix her face. She did everything slowly and deliberately, and all the time the question was hammering in her brain, 'What am I going to do? What am I going to *do*?'

She looked fine when she had finished, but she still sat at the dressing table, her hands lying limp before her with a ring on every finger. If Martin had noticed the thickest ring on the third finger of her left hand he hadn't remarked on it. Nobody had.

There was a knock on the door and she called, 'I'm ready, I'm coming!' and her father opened the door. Lacey had expected Paul. She told him when she left him downstairs that she would be about ten minutes and she had been up here a good half hour.

Her father stood in the doorway, breathing hard, his face flushed to a mottled scarlet, and Lacey jumped up.

'Let me sit down.' He took a chair by the door and went on panting. She had never seen him looking so rattled. He was a man who usually allowed nothing to disturb him, but something had got right under his skin this time, and it was probably Martin.

'What's the matter?' she asked. 'Is it Martin Jackson?'

'Yes. Oh yes, it's Martin Jackson. Paul's just told me you're cooking four meals for him and he's staying for the full two weeks of the festival.'

'Yes.' That would hardly seem to explain why her father should be steaming under the collar. She heard herself say flippantly, 'I'm cooking for him, not sleeping with him,' and a shocked expression settled on Laurence Allen's face that made her want to smile. He was a great artist, but he was out of touch with the changing times. She said, 'Sorry. But it's true, so what's the worry?'

'His father was a good friend of mine,' said her father. 'I knew a great deal about that young man that wasn't common knowledge.'

'I know you never liked him.' She had thought that was because Martin had never been impressed by her father, but her father said suddenly and harshly,

'He killed my old friend.'

She winced, 'That's a terrible thing to say!' but Laurence Allen was implacable,

'He died of a heart attack and he was never strong physically, but his son shortened his life. I can never forget that, nor forgive it.'

'What did Martin *do*?' She remembered Courtney Jackson as a highly respected retired stockbroker. Martin had always been on the wild side and there must have been times when he and his father didn't see eye to eye. But academically Martin was brilliant. Most men, she felt, would have been proud of him as a son.

The ruddy colour was fading from her father's face. He was looking drawn now. 'Courtney Jackson was a broken man when he died. He told me things I don't think he ever told anyone else. Do you know what he said to me?' She shook her head. 'He said,' said her father, ' "My son has no feeling for anyone but himself. He's ruthless and he'll get to the top, but I think he was born without a heart." He said he wouldn't be seeing Martin again now that the money had gone. Martin had it, the money; I think there was forgery there. A few days after that Courtney Jackson had a heart attack in the High Street and died.'

Lacey turned her head, feeling sick. After a moment she said, 'I asked him to dinner tomorrow night.'

'Not to my house,' said her father.

'No.' Not at the table where her father had eaten with his old friend, nor in the rooms where Martin's father had talked like a broken man a few days before his death.

'I'd rather you didn't have to see him at all.' Her father got up and put a hand on her shoulder as though he needed her support. 'Send them a cheque for this hiring mop nonsense and keep out of his way. He's a contamination. It was hard enough shaking hands and talking civilly to him this morning. I hadn't realised how meeting him again would affect me. I won't breathe the same air as him again if I can help it, and I don't want you having to either.'

'All right,' she said, and the thought struck her that what her father had heard in confidence would be slander if he repeated it now. 'Does Paul know?'

'Not what I've just told you.'

'Don't tell anybody else.'

He looked affronted. 'Don't you believe me?'

'Of course I do,' she said quickly, 'but if it got around that you were accusing Martin of swindling his father, and you did say that, didn't you? I mean, I don't suppose anything could be proved after all this time and—well, he could sue you, couldn't he?'

'And he would,' said Laurence Allen grimly. 'You're quite right, my dear. You're going out with Paul, are you?'

As Paul was waiting downstairs while she was changing up here that was obvious. She said, 'Yes,' and her father said, 'Now there's a very different cut of young man,' as though that comforted him.

She said, 'Yes,' again, and reached for a perfume atomiser that Paul had given her only last week and sprayed herself liberally. That was a sad and sordid little tale. Perhaps it showed that her instincts had been sound even as a child. There had always been this conflict, she had always sensed that Martin Jackson was dangerous, and his father, who must have known him best, had apparently believed with proof that Martin had no feeling for anyone but himself.

Paul *was* different. Fond of his family and friends and kind to them, there was nothing ruthless about Paul. He was a tender and considerate lover and she would stay close to him so long as Martin was in town; and if she came across Martin again she would remember what her father had just told her.

Her father coughed, as the cloud of perfume irritated his throat, then he sighed and said he thought he would have an early night. He had intended going out to dinner, but today had been rather exhausting so he would have a cold supper, read a little and then go to bed.

'You are all right?' He had seemed very shaken. Lacey had had no idea how strong his prejudices were against Martin. Today must have been a real ordeal for him, and she continued to look anxiously at him while he reassured her as they came downstairs.

Paul was still sitting in front of the television in the drawing room. 'Did you see it?' he asked Lacey.

'What? Oh, the opening. Oh yes—good, wasn't it? I really will be with you in a minute, I'm just going to fix a supper tray for my father.' She was putting out cold meat, chutney and cheese, with a half bottle of wine, when she remembered that she had invited Paul back here to tea. So she switched on the kettle and started preparing a second tray, with half a Dundee cake and a plate of ham sandwiches.

She wasn't hungry herself. She was finding all this food stomach churning. It had been a long day for her too, she felt as if she had been put through a wringer; and left to herself, with no one to please but herself, she would probably have gone to bed and pulled the sheets over her head. But Paul was still waiting, and after he had drunk his tea and eaten most of the sandwiches and a large slice of cake they said goodbye to her father and walked out of the house.

Chadsford was lit up. Streets were festooned with fairy lights that were part of the annual Christmas display and most shops and hotels had gone to town on their decorative illuminations. There was open air dancing to a local student group in the town square, and from a meadow just outside town came the raucous cacophony of a funfair. It was all so dramatically different from the usual quiet of evening that Lacey stopped and stared.

She had started this. It had all sprung from her casual remark about the hiring mop, and it was lovely. Everybody was having fun and it was altogether a marvellous idea. But she felt as though she had put a match to a barrel of fireworks which was going off merrily, all shooting stars and colourful lights, and she was the only one who knew about the stick of dynamite at the bottom of the barrel.

Paul was asking her, 'What are you doing about tomorrow? Only he seemed very upset when I told him that Jackson was staying on and about the hiring. He wanted to know why I didn't stop it.' He gave a short embarrassed laugh, 'He was carrying on as though you'd been sold into white slavery, and he didn't give me a chance to explain that I wasn't there before he went storming off. I've never seen him so put out about anything, but he did seem to have calmed down when you came downstairs.'

'He had his say,' said Lacey. 'And there's a fair chance that if Martin eats here tomorrow my father could poison him.'

'That bad?' Paul was smiling broadly. He knew how strong her father's influence was over Lacey and he was glad that Laurence Allen's antipathy for Martin Jackson hadn't softened with the years. 'You did say you'd phone and warn him not to come if your father was against it,' he reminded Lacey.

'I will,' she said.

'Are you carrying on cooking the meals for him?'

She could have said no, because she wasn't, but she heard herself say, 'We'll see,' and stepped out, walking down the hill towards the lights of the town.

There was entertainment on, from poetry readings in pubs to a concert of chamber music by members of the local Philharmonic Society. The streets were crowded. In town the focal point was the square where four young students from the local Poly, one on the drums, two with guitars, and a singer, were belting out their music on a stage of the town hall steps. Amplifiers magnified the sound and distorted the words, but the sound was the thing.

The square was full of dancers. Some Lacey knew, some were strangers, and the beat of the music was getting to her. It was carnival time, and she felt like dancing. She waved at a couple of friends whirling by and caught Paul's hand. 'Come on!' she urged him.

Lacey was a good dancer, light on her feet and with a sense of rhythm. She hadn't danced for a long time because Paul was no dancer, but in this crowd all he needed to do was move. Lacey danced fast, as though she could throw off her worries, and lose herself in the music. She twirled and whirled, smiling at friends and strangers.

Nearly everybody was smiling. A good time was being had by nearly everybody, but Paul looked uncomfortably stiff and selfconscious, his shoulders jerking up and down while Lacey tried to guide him through the steps. She wondered how Martin would dance, remembering the animal grace of his movements, and she found herself scanning faces.

She was sure Martin was out here somewhere, and wondered if Denice was still with him. Or following him around, as she used to do in the old days. So had half the girls who had grown up with Lacey. Martin had broken a fair number of hearts before he left town for good.

Paul stepped back and collided with a girl whose carrot red hair was teased into a spiky halo, and whose cheekbones were outlined with green stars. 'Whoops!' she shrieked, and then fell about laughing when she recognised him. 'Fancy meeting you! Bit of all right, isn't it? Nice if we could have this every Saturday night.'

She was one of the juniors in the library, transmogrified in disco warpaint, and as she jived away Paul mutterd, 'I've had enough of this, making a spectacle of myself,' and pushed his way through the dancers to the far end of the square.

Lacey followed, but when she stepped on to the side path she protested, 'I was enjoying myself.'

'Don't let me stop you.' Paul sounded huffy. 'But don't you think you should be leaving that message telling Jackson not to turn up at your father's house tomorrow?'

My house too, she thought, my home. 'I'll get round to it,' she said. 'Don't nag me.'

'I've never nagged anybody in my life.' Somehow she was managing to offend him and somehow, for the first time, he was managing to get on her nerves. 'But if your father feels this strongly——' he went on, and she remembered how Aunt Helena used to say, 'Your father is a great artist and his work is the most important thing in this house.' In short, his wishes come first every time.

'Have no fear,' she said in throbbing tones. 'Martin Jackson will never darken my father's door.' She made it sound like a line from the melodrama, and Paul scowled, and at that moment Porteus and Maisie strolled by, arm in arm, and Maisie called, 'Coming to the fair?'

'I can't stand fairgrounds,' Paul muttered, and Lacey said silkily,

'Ah, had enough excitement for one night? Mind if I go?'

'You please yourself,' said Paul. 'I wouldn't dream of nagging you.'

She would be apologising tomorrow, but tonight she could have shaken him. She wanted him to smile with her, to *enjoy* things, to share in the fun and stop the dark fears from coming out of the shadows and overwhelming her.

'Right,' she said. 'Dinner tomorrow? My place?'

'Thank you,' said Paul, not sounding all that grateful, and she slipped her hand through Porteus's other arm and said, 'Come on, let's go to the fair.'

Porteus and Maisie had heard about the hiring mop, and they would have had to be very obtuse not to have sensed the atmosphere here. As soon as they were out of Paul's hearing Maisie demanded incredulously, 'Have you two had a tiff?'

'I don't know.' Lacey never argued, much less quarrelled with Paul. 'I think perhaps we have.'

'Not over Martin Jackson?' Maisie knew about the old days, and it was a shaker if Martin Jackson and Lacey should be getting together, the last thing anybody would have expected.

'I think,' said Lacey, 'it was over me wanting to dance in the square and Paul deciding it was a public spectacle.'

'Well, of course it's a public spectacle,' boomed Porteus. 'That's the idea, isn't it? A free-for-all.' A student rattled a collecting box for Oxfam under their noses and they dropped in coins, and Lacey beamed,

'Isn't the High Street pretty? Our own Golden Mile.'

The fair was pitched in a five-acre field just out of town and the crowds were streaming towards it. A roller-coaster and a big wheel and a helter-skelter rose high overhead; roundabouts and various bone-shaking rides whirled around in what seemed to be perpetual motion. There were all the usual sideshows and stalls and Lacey said, 'Hi', to a lot of people including a photographer and reporter from the *Chadsford Mercury*.

When they reached the Ghost Train Maisie declared, 'Oh, I love Ghost Trains!' There was only room for two in a car, if one was as broad in the beam as Porteus, so Lacey said, 'See you tomorrow,' and waved them off into the black tunnel. She could soon find a companion if she wanted company, although wandering around by herself was pleasant enough. What she should be doing, she supposed, was leaving that message for Martin, but she could do that tomorrow morning. She wasn't putting it off. It was just that there was no hurry.

She saw him straight ahead of her, tall enough to tower over the crowds. His head was turned. She caught him in profile, and she ducked back into the first opening that offered cover—a sideshow billed as The World of Mirrors. Inside distorting mirrors were arranged strategically to give an illusion of rooms and passages, and grinning fairgoers were undulating in front of them vying with each other to make the most grotesque reflections.

Lacey went through the biggest room, along a passage, and stopped at the end of that, facing a mirror that made her body into a squat little dwarf with a neck like a giraffe and on top of the neck a thin elongated face. She let out her breath; she must have been holding it. She did not want to meet Martin, with or without Denice. Now she knew he was in the fairground, she would get out of it as soon as she had given him time to pass by. She stood, arms folded, looking at the monstrosity in the mirror, and another caricature of a face appeared over hers.

She had heard soft footsteps on the grass. She didn't turn. She asked the face in the mirror, 'What brings you in here?'

'What brings you?' Martin countered.

'I was dodging you.'

'Makes sense. I was following you.'

She didn't think he had seen her, but he must have done. 'Why?' she asked.

'Am I still coming to dinner tomorrow?'

'No.'

'I didn't think I would be.'

She turned then, and there was nobody behind him in this little cul-de-sac, although he might have left them in front of other mirrors. 'Well, it surprised me,' she said. 'I never thought my father would care much one way or the other, but it seems he does.'

'Are you by yourself?' He moved back a step to let her by and then followed close behind, and she resisted the urge to start running.

'I came with some friends, but we got separated,' she told him. She walked towards the exit. Outside the music seemed to blare louder than ever and the lights were fierce and dazzling. 'Who's with you?' she asked.

'You are, aren't you?' Martin was holding her hand, their fingers laced, and she had neither the strength nor the will to pull away. Her lips began to smile and the smile spread through her warming as wine, relaxing the tension. She felt the pressure of his thumb on the palm of her hand, insistent and intimate, and she said, 'A fairground suits you, you know. You look the part.'

He looked younger than he had this morning, the lines in his face seemed less deep. 'The smile suits you,' he said, and they began to walk together between the stalls.

Here's a carry-on, Lacey thought. This is what we should have done five years ago. It was like a time-warp, as though she was nineteen again, and he was twenty-two, and they would meet friends who would gasp, not believing their own eyes seeing Martin and Lacey, strolling around together?

'Candy floss or brandy snaps?' he asked.

'Brandy snaps.' She took the bag. It felt warm, the smell was sweet and nutty. A fortune-teller's tent was next to the sweetmeats stall, and she glanced up at the row of framed photographs of celebrities with 'Rosita, seer to the stars'.

'I don't see you,' she said.

'Never felt the need of it, but you've got a lucky face, lady—have your palm read.'

'I don't need it either, I know my fortune.'

'Oh?'

She had to say this. 'You've met Paul.'

'Yes, but I don't see him around.' He wasn't looking around, he was looking down at her.

'He's—er—working.' Paul might have followed them to the fair, but she didn't think so.

'What about him?' asked Martin.

'He's my future.' Martin burst out laughing, and she was half laughing herself although she insisted, 'He *is*,' then she shrugged, 'Ah, forget it.'

'Good idea,' he said. 'How do you feel about the dodgems?'

'Why not?'

'Or the big wheel?'

'Let's ride high,' she said.

The carriages were small and enclosed, with room for two a side, but no one joined them, and they sat facing each other as the wheel started up again, and then the carriages began their sweep of rise and descent. From the top you got a fantastic view, through the meshed windows, of the fair with all its lights just below and the brightly lit-up streets of the town. They picked out places here and there. Where the Arts Centre was. The floodlit square, enclosing the moving mosaic of dancers.

If Paul goes back to his flat, thought Lacey, he won't get much peace this side of midnight; and she wondered what Paul would say if he could see her, up here with Martin.

'Are you really staying the fortnight?' she asked.

'Of course.'

'Well, watch it with Denice. That marriage isn't too solid, you could be all that's needed to blow it.'

'Thanks for the warning.' They were going up now, he was still scanning the scene below, the higher they went the smaller the people looked and more insignificant, and she said,

'She's a nice girl.' Denice's infatuation for Martin Jackson had been pathetic and ridiculous, but she was a nice girl.

'She's a fool,' he said callously. 'She always was,' and Lacey snapped,

'Is that what you thought about all of us? Small town folk with small town minds?'

'Is that what you thought you were?' Martin still looked out of the window, and it seemed to her that they were losing speed, moving in slower motion, that each word had become deliberate and loaded. She said,

'Well, this place wasn't big enough to hold you, was it?'

'There was nothing in it to hold me,' he said, and she told him savagely,

'My father said you killed his old friend.'

'What old friend?'

'Your father.'

'He's out of his mind!'

'With worry,' he said. 'Your father worried about you.'

'Could be, I suppose.' His face was inscrutable, heavy-lidded. 'I didn't see myself following his line of business. I didn't see myself following him in anything.'

Mr Jackson must have wanted Martin to be a stockbroker, and Martin had had his own ideas and chosen his own career. That was understandable. But it chilled her that he expressed no regret at all. If anyone had told her even years afterwards that her selfishness had hastened anybody's death she would have been conscience-stricken. Her father had said he was heartless, and she spoke into the hush that had descended on them, 'Don't you feel anything about that? Don't you have any feelings?'

There *was* a hush. No creaking, no sound of machinery. And then the carriage lurched like a bucking bronco and there were shouts and shrieks, and she was hurled straight at Martin, spreadeagled across him, and the carriage shuddered and they were in a huddle on the floor, and now he was on top of her.

Her screams were choked. His arms were around her and he was kissing her with a wild passion that blotted out everything else. Then he jerked his head back. 'How about you? Do you have feelings? Did you feel that?'

He wasn't talking about the mechanical failure that had brought the big wheel to a halt. The carriage was steady now, but her heart was racing because she had gone out of her mind. She would have stayed in his arms, mouth to mouth, clinging to him, if the whole darn shoot had gone crashing down.

CHAPTER THREE

LACEY began to laugh. The laughter bubbled up in her and she hoped it wasn't hysteria, but she wasn't sure. 'I've heard about the earth shaking, but this is ridiculous,' she said.

They still lay together, in the little dusty space between the seats, and Martin's arms were still tight around her. He grinned, she saw the whiteness of his teeth in the dark tan of his face. 'We do our lovemaking with some interesting backgrounds,' he said. 'We could do a sexy disaster movie.'

He was remembering the last time, the only time. This had stopped at kissing so far, and Lacey wriggled to sit up. 'What happened?'

'Not a lot,' he said. That was what he thought. Too much had happened to her. She knew now that she was vulnerable, that the old magic still worked. She slid from under him on to the seat. 'This isn't part of the ride, is it?'

'I shouldn't think it's a scheduled stop,' he said gravely, and the shouting was a chorus, everybody yelling, 'What's going on?' Then a louder voice over a speaker, soothing, almost jovial, telling them all to keep calm, that this was just a minor fault. Nobody was in any danger, and they would all be brought down safely and smoothly within a few minutes.

'No hurry, mate,' said Martin, getting up off the floor.

Their carriage was the highest. 'Well, we got the best seats,' said Lacey. 'Right at the top. Do you feel at home up here?'

'Very cosy.' He sat down beside her. There were brandy snaps all over the place, but a few were left in the bottom of the bag, and she offered him the bag.

'Iron rations too. Here they are. Here's the first meal I owe you.' He was going to take her in his arms again, but she jumped up and he said, 'Sit down, you're rocking the boat.'

She sat on the opposite seat, pressing her spine against the back, feet tucked under, arms folded and hands gripping her upper arms, so that there was no way she would brush against him. That way she felt safer, and her voice sounded as steady as his. 'No, I'm not, and I don't want the boat rocked.'

'Sure of that?' She knew his eyes were blue, but they looked black, up here in the shadows.

'Very, very sure,' she said, and dragged her gaze away and looked out at the flurry of activity down there on the ground. The rest of the fair didn't seem to be affected. Music was still blaring and all the other rides appeared to be working. Only the big wheel was stationary. 'I suppose we shall be rescued,' she mused. 'What if the works have really seized up? It's a long way down. I've seen films where they jump from carriage to carriage, but I never fancied it myself.'

'A fireman's ladder or a helicopter?' Martin suggested. 'Any preference?' and she laughed.

'That would be making a public spectacle of myself.'

'Who cares?' He had never cared. He had always done what he wanted to do.

'Some people,' she said, and thought of Paul and bit her lip, because Paul would want an apology for this. This would not be easy to explain.

'Where did you get all the rings?' Martin asked.

'I bought them.'

'Sell me one.'

'They wouldn't fit you.' One of the bigger ones might, he had thin strong hands, but she had never seen him wearing rings, or any jewellery, and when he caught her hand and began to ease off the ring on her third finger she bunched her fingers into a fist and jerked it away.

'You can buy one for yourself,' she said. 'You know the stall, you saw it this morning. They'll do you a special design if you like.'

She wished they would get this thing moving. If she was stuck up here much longer with Martin she could make such a fool of herself.

'How does it do, your Arts Centre?' he asked.

'Most of us make a living.'

'You're happy, are you?' He could always get people talking, sometimes saying things they would rather have kept quiet. This was no T.V. interview, and she could have answered easily enough, because of course she was happy. But she didn't reply at once, and he went on quietly, 'Settled? Satisfied? Never felt like breaking away and following your star?'

'What star?' Her restlessness had been curbed from an early age. He was the restless one, the world was his stalking ground. Wherever he went there was excitement and adventure, and she made herself laugh again to stop this conversation becoming serious. 'I'm nearer the stars right now,' she joked, 'than I've been for a long time.'

She was feeling more alive than she had felt for a long time. She could deny it all she liked, but when Martin was near her blood tingled. His eyes on her were more disturbing than the touch of another man's hands.

'What's your perfume?' he asked.

Paul's gift, chosen and given with love. It was sweet and sometimes she found it a little cloying. 'It isn't right for you,' said Martin.

'Yes, it is, and how would you know what's right for me?' She was stung because Paul knew her so well. Over the last two years they had discussed everything under the sun. She had told Paul her thoughts, her hopes, her fears. She had told Martin so little, and that five years ago during one night.

'I do know,' he said.

He recognised, as she did, the powerful physical pull

between them. No more, no deeper, certainly nothing of the spirit. It was pure lust, but the attraction he had for her was terrifying. She ached to reach out and run her hands over his shoulders, under the shirt, tracing collar bones beneath the skin, and the hard muscles of his back; or to dig her fingers into the thick dark curling hair and pull his face down to hers.

She started to talk about the Arts Centre, giving him potted biographies of the people who worked and sold there. He had met most of them this morning. Some of them he had known when he lived in Chadsford, others had arrived in town after he left, but there was enough to tell to fill the next ten minutes, and then the carriage gave a little judder and a cheering went up.

'We're away,' said Martin.

They moved with pauses, as the carriages emptied one by one, and the released joyriders began stumbling out. Lacey watched them, all fortunately seemed young and agile. Any brittle bones might have fared badly in the shake-up, but so far nobody was being lifted out.

Martin pulled her from the window and kissed her again, slower, deeper, and she thought wildly, 'He's left it too late to rape me,' and mumbled, 'Have you gone crazy?'

'I never felt saner.' Theirs would be the next carriage to touch down. He held her face between his cupped hands and she said,

'We'd better walk out, not fall out, don't you think?'

'However you like.'

The local press photographer had been taking pictures for a centre page spread on the first night of the festival. He had spent the last five minutes on action shots around the immobilised big wheel. Now he was clicking away as the riders emerged, and Martin Jackson, a celebrity, stepping out, was a nice little scoop. Lacey Allen was quite well known locally too, and their photograph would certainly grace next Friday's *Mercury*.

Brenda Brown, the earnest young reporter with pad poised, blinked owlishly behind her round-rimmed spectacles and asked what they'd thought when the wheel stopped turning.

'It was a wonderful view,' said Lacey. 'Wasn't it Martin?'

'Fantastic,' said Martin, and grinned at Miss Brown, who blinked again and smiled back and started to breathe faster. Lacey saw with horror that Martin had a smear of her lipstick on his face, and knew he wouldn't care, and was conscious of dirt on her dress where she had landed full-length on the floor, then squirmed out from under Martin. Although that was unlikely to show up in the press photograph, any more than the lipstick was, the two things added up, and Charlie Rilke, the photographer, was grinning from ear to ear.

'Got badly shaken up, did you?' he was asking.

'Badly enough,' said Lacey, trying to sound dignified.

'It was nearly a quarter of an hour before they fixed it. Did you begin to wonder whether they'd be getting you down tonight?'

Charlie knew Paul, but he was a cynical little man who admired Martin Jackson. 'You know, we never got round to wondering about that,' said Martin. He sounded serious, but Charlie went on grinning. 'What with this fantastic view,' said Martin, 'we hardly seemed to be up there any time at all.'

There was laughter, and another carriage was emptying, and Lacey darted into the crowd hurrying away. 'You've got lipstick on your cheek' she hissed at Martin who was still beside her. He rubbed. 'The other cheek,' she snapped, 'and you can leave me now, because I'm going home.'

'I'll walk with you.'

'I don't need——' She didn't need and she didn't want, but she knew that she wasn't going to get away from him until she actually closed a door, so she kept her head down and walked fast, not even talking unless she had to. Even when he directed a remark at her she said nothing unless it was a question, and then she answered as briefly as possible.

They passed friends. There was more than one astonished, 'Hello, what are you two doing together?' and Lacey would say, 'Sorry, but I've got to rush, I'm late,' although it sounded rude and Martin knew it was a lie. She just went on, and she was sure they would try to stop him, but he always caught up with her, so he couldn't have exchanged more than a few words before he was on her track again.

Well, he'd gain nothing from it. She *was* going home, and hers was probably the only house in town where he wouldn't get over the threshold. At the gate she said, 'You can't come in.'

'I know that.'

'Then go away.' They didn't often close the gate. It was Victorian ironwork with scrolls and bars and the bottom of it scraped the gravel as she dragged it to. She talked to him through the bars. 'I never wanted you to come back here, I had a feeling you'd cause trouble. Well, you're causing none for me, so goodnight—and I'd very much like it to be goodbye.'

He said, 'I don't believe you.'

'God, you are so conceited!' He knew the sexual attraction he had for her. And for ninety-nine women in a hundred, she suspected. It must have been a challenge to him when they were both younger, that she was the one girl who showed how she disliked him. When she became the last scalp he collected in this town that must have given him an ego-boost. He had gone away, and never looked back, but he must have smiled at how easy that seduction was, how quickly and completely Lacey Allen had gone up in flames.

And the awful thing was that after five long years the sensual spell was still as potent. But it was a black magic and she was not letting it enslave her.

'See you,' said Martin, and as he turned away from the gate she said, 'No.'

'Yes.' He looked back, over his shoulder, eyes hard, mouth unsmiling, and she wanted to scream, 'No!' again. She hated him. She really hated him. So sure of himself that he could believe that five years later she was still here for the taking.

She let herself into the house, shutting the heavy front door quietly because she couldn't face her father tonight. He would want to know where Paul was, and she couldn't start to explain what had happened. Tomorrow would be too soon, tonight was impossible. There was a thin thread of light showing round the drawing room door, and she hurried up the stairs to her bedroom.

Through the open window she could still hear the sounds of the fair, and see the glow in the sky. They would be dancing in the square until midnight. If she tried she could pick out the music blaring through the loudspeakers there from the general babel, and she closed the window and pulled the curtains.

In Paul's flat, overlooking the square, there would be no shutting out the music, but if she had been sure he was at home she might have gone there. Running for cover. Suppose she had said to Paul, 'He's after me. That's why I didn't want him coming back. For years we had a running battle, but the last night he was here we were lovers, and that was incredible. That was so right I couldn't believe it. Then he went away. We never wrote to each other, nor phoned, we never saw each other again. It was a one-night one-off for him and I thought I'd forgotten, but when I'm near him I'm crying out for him. I know it wouldn't be love. It's you I love. With him it's madness, but every inch of me aches for him so that I could weep from the pain.'

If she said one tenth of that to Paul she would lose him for ever. This was an infatuation like poor Denice, like others. Martin Jackson had animal sensuality to an almost criminal degree. He should be locked away. He shouldn't be let loose.

She hadn't switched on the lights. She kicked off her shoes and sat on the bed, hands looped around her ankles, chin on her knees, until her eyes were used to the dark and she could have moved around the room without bumping into anything. But she didn't move. She sat quite still, reliving a darker night . . .

It was summer hot, like tonight. Hotter, more oppressive. Everybody was waiting for the weather to break as day followed day of blue skies and sunshine. 'This can't go on,' everybody had been saying for the last five weeks, and that night the clouds were gathering, blotting out the stars. The air was still and thick and heavy, and thunder was growling like a beast prowling.

Her father had been up to London for the day, come back tired and gone to bed early, but downstairs in the drawing room Aunt Helena was working on a piece of tapestry. The house was still full of Aunt Helena's tapestries. Most of them featured birds, they had been a lifetime's hobby, and there were other houses all over the country where old friends had cushions and firescreens and framed pictures, all exquisitely worked by Aunt Helena. That night it had been a tropical bird of paradise, with feathers of purple and cerise. It had ended as a Christmas present and still hung in a drawing room where Lacey had tea from time to time. If she could she always sat with her back to it.

That night it was only half complete, stretched on a frame, and Aunt Helena's needle had stabbed in and out all the time Lacey was talking. 'I'm not good enough,' Lacey had said, 'it's just a waste going on.'

She was at the local art college then, and this was her own opinion of her work, because her tutors seemed content to continue to teach her, and there were other students happily producing worse. But during the summer holidays Lacey had become increasingly dissatisfied. She was at the end of a romance, but it wasn't affecting her deeply, she was the one calling the halt, but she had been considering dropping out of her arts course. She was nineteen and she wanted to see something of the world.

Her father had no idea. It was Aunt Helena who watched Lacey's moods and who was listening to this outburst, stitching, her needle catching flashes of light. When Lacey stopped talking Aunt Helena said quietly, 'I'm an old woman. I won't be with you much longer. Your father is going to need you.'

Lacey had been reared to that, and perhaps this feeling that life was passing her by was only a temporary depression. Life was almost over for Aunt Helena, with her bottles of prescription pills. Her face was greying now and Lacey knew that the little scene had distressed her. She hurried for the panic pills and Helena Allen swallowed a couple of them with sips of water, closed her eyes for a moment, then smiled wanly at Lacey as though saying, 'You see?'

Lacey saw. She believed that she loved her father as much as his sister did, and she loved Aunt Helena too. She said, 'We'll give it another term. See how things look around Christmas. Of course there isn't much else I'm trained for. Except keeping house.'

'One genius in the family is enough.' Aunt Helena's smile was gay now, almost girlish, and Lacey knew that she could never leave them. She made hot milky nightcaps, put one on a table beside her aunt's chair, and carried her own to the sofa, sitting with a book for a while. There was music on the radio that crackled occasionally. They had turned off the television because Aunt Helena was always apprehensive about that when there was a threat of storm, and surely the storm was going to break before long.

Lacey wished it would. Her nerves felt like tightening wires, and the elegant familiar room, with Aunt Helena at her tapestry, even the soft background music, seemed to be closing in on her. She shut her book, the printed words were dancing on the page, that could be a warning of a migraine, and said, 'I think I'm going to bed.'

'I'll stay down a little longer.' Aunt Helena took up another hank of silk—dark green this time—and rethreaded a needle. Her eyes were sharp and clear. She needed heart pills, but not spectacles. She missed nothing that might interfere with Laurence Allen's comfort, and she truly believed that Lacey's happiness lay in helping to run this house while he painted his pictures.

At the door of her bedroom Lacey changed her mind, and instead tiptoed downstairs again and out of the house. She was suffocating. The air was so heavy she could hardly breathe. Out of doors it was just as still and the streets were empty. There was not a sign of life, except for lights here and there. The town could be dead. She could be the only one left alive, and she was in soft-soled pumps that hardly made a sound.

She walked through the streets, breathing shallowly, not to shatter the silence, although that was crazy; and she came to the Jacksons' house, about five minutes' walk from her own house. It was a three-storeyed Georgian, opening on to the pavement, and the For Sale notice was up in a ground floor window. Courtney Jackson had died four months before; his sudden death from a heart attack was always in Lacey's mind when Aunt Helena looked unwell. No one lived here now. Last week there had been an auction of contents, but as she reached the front door it opened and Martin came out.

He almost collided with her. They weaved, side-stepping, and stopped, facing each other. He asked, 'What are you doing?' and she answered, flippantly because that was the way the words came,

'Walking. No law against it, is there?'

He shrugged, 'None that I know.'

Lacey turned her head towards the notice in the window, 'Sorry—about that.' She hadn't gone to the auction, although everybody else seemed to have done. The For Sale notice on the house had gone up after the auction. Big black letters on the blank window, and behind, an echoing house. She wondered what he was doing in there, although of course some furniture must have been left. It was still his home. They walked from the house, side by side, down the empty pavement. 'Going anywhere in particular?' he asked.

She shook her head. 'Are you?'

'Over the hills.'

Nothing else was said. They left the road for a track on to the common. Lacey took no notice of him, nor he of her. She went at her own pace, picking her own path, and when she stumbled on uneven ground he made no move to catch her, although he was only an arm's length away.

They were deep in their own thoughts. She wouldn't have been on the moors alone this late, but in every respect but the physical they *were* alone. There was no word and no contact between them. If the storm broke perhaps the silence would. Or they might just walk and go back and say nothing but goodnight.

The thunder was rolling closer, and the lightning flashes were throwing weird blue lights over the countryside. At the top of a hill, looking down into a clearing skirted by pine trees, Lacey stopped. Her head was throbbing and iron bands seemed clamped round her chest as the frustration and despair that had been building up became overwhelming. She was a prisoner. Caged. Because her father was a great artist and she was nothing but his daughter.

A sound like a sob burst from her, although it was only a gasp for air. At least she thought it was, and Martin asked, 'What's the matter?'

'Nothing.'

'Then what's this?' He wiped her cheek with the flat of his hand and it came away wet and she said,

'It's raining.' She could feel the tears now, and his hands on her shoulders. Her head fell back and a raindrop landed on her nose. 'How's that for on cue?' he said, and his hands slipped down so that his arms were around her, hugging her, and they were both laughing, faces upturned, when the heavens opened.

'We must be out of our minds, coming out here!' Martin spluttered. It was like standing under a waterfall, and Lacey felt a wild exhilaration,

'No, it's lovely. I don't care if it washes me away.'

No more did she. The rain was dissolving the tears and the tension. She felt clean and free, and when Martin grinned at her and said, 'You're a crazy wench,' she laughed with him.

'I'm crazy? Whose idea was this anyway, walking over the hills?'

He was wearing a grey bomber jacket, which he unzipped and put over her. although it was too late to do any good, then they ran, slithering down the hill. In those days, the old charcoal burner's hut still had a door and a roof. There were holes in both, but the hut was sheltered under the trees, and when they stumbled inside it seemed a welcoming refuge. The floor was turf, carpet-soft, and it was warm in here and the rain hardly reached them.

Lacey was wearing an Indian cotton caftan in lilacs and rose pink, and as she had been drenched to the skin before Martin had put his jacket on her, she was as wet as he was. His grey shirt was clinging to him and his hair was a wild halo.

That was what happened to her hair when it was wet, it curled to a frizz, that was how it must look now. 'You've got my kind of hair,' she said. 'Isn't it a nuisance?'

'On you it looks good.' He ruffled her hair and a little shiver of pleasure went down her spine. Suddenly her legs were weak, what with walking and getting caught in the storm, and her knees gave way and she was sitting on her heels. Martin sat down beside her, cradling her against him, and she curled her legs more comfortably and settled her head on his shoulder.

Everything seemed new, and easy. As if there were no problems that she couldn't solve. She felt strong and confident, watching the storm and talking, talking, talking. She had always known that Martin Jackson was good company. She had been in company with him, but they had never been alone together before, yet now it seemed the most natural thing in the world, and her old defensiveness against him was only a dim memory.

He talked about Cambridge; he had already been offered entry into television as a graduate news trainee when he left college. Lacey had heard that already. He told her about fellow students and she saw them vividly, and felt that she would have recognised them if she had come across them. She talked of art college and he said, 'I hear you're the sex symbol of your year.'

'I hear about you too,' she said. 'It would be hard not to. You always did get yourself talked about.' This time there was no barb in that. She leaned back on his arm looking at his face, and liking what she saw because it had something the other men and boys had lacked.

'Got a lot in common, haven't we?' he said. 'Besides the hairstyle.' He had to be joking. They were poles apart. His mother had died when he was born, hers before she could remember, but compared with him her achievements were nil. Now she laughed, 'Oh, we're out of the same mould. Could be brother and sister, we could.'

Her eyes were light blue, his were dark, and her mouth had none of the hardness of his. She couldn't look away from his mouth.

'No,' he said, 'not brother and sister. Siblings maybe, way back.' They were not related, but she felt an affinity with him, sitting in this little hut with the storm all around, as though he was the best friend she would ever have.

A mighty crash of thunder made them jump and they smiled at each other and, still smiling, were suddenly quiet. Then Martin began to touch her, tracing brows and cheekbones and lips, running his hands over her warm skin beneath the damp clinging cotton, as though he was not sure if she was real.

An explosion of sensation followed his touch, a reaction she had never imagined in her wildest dreams. Instinctively her arms opened, and she clung to him fiercely as they kissed, drawing him down with her. She couldn't have turned away. There was no holding back, no hesitation. Nothing had ever felt so incredible to her as this overwhelming natural force, as though they rode the storm together, higher and higher, into a climax of delight beyond time and space. And then a blurring of the senses, free-falling, floating down on to the soft turf, and still the closeness as though she would never be alone again.

She slept and woke in Martin's arms. When she opened her eyes and saw him beside her there was no surprise. That felt natural too, there was no shock to jolt her. She was relaxed and sleepy, and she yawned and stretched and said, 'Morning.'

'Not quite.' It was still dark, although his face was close and clear. She felt the warmth of him and she could hear her own heart beating. 'Has it stopped raining?' The trees were rustling, but the sound of storm seemed to have died away.

'Getting its breath back,' he said. 'There've been lulls before then it's started again.'

Lacey wondered how long he had been awake, if he had slept at all, and sat up. 'I must get home.'

'Do they know you're out?'

'With luck, no.' She had said goodnight and Aunt Helena was unlikely to look into her room. But if she did and Lacey was missing for hours there would be a general alarm. Lacey scrambled to her feet. 'What time is it?'

'Coming up to three. Look, I've got to leave early tomorrow—today. I'll phone you.'

'Yes,' she said. She scrabbled on the turf for shoes and pulled her thin clothing around her. 'Lord, I hope they haven't missed me. It would be enough to give Aunt Helena——' Just in time she remembered his father and didn't say a 'heart attack.' 'An awful shock,' she said.

It began to rain again as they hurried across the moorlands. Nothing like the first drenching downpour, but soft and steady and chilling. Martin had her arm now, they were together every step, and when they reached his house and she said, 'I'll be all right from here,' he said,

'I'll take you home.'

She was praying that the lights wouldn't be on. With the rain and the trees it was hard to tell, although the house stood high. She couldn't be sure until they were almost at the gate, she had run all the way up the hill, and she was breathless and panting. 'It looks all right,' she said, limp with relief. 'Goodbye.'

'Goodbye.' She couldn't be absolutely certain until she had opened the front door and seen no lights towards the rear of the house. From looking into the darkened hall she turned back to the gate where she had left him. She had thought he would stand there and see her in. She had raised a hand to wave, but he had gone.

That made sense, it was still raining. Lacey hoped there was still hot water in his house, and she crept into the bathroom and ran a hot bath for herself. It wouldn't have mattered at this stage if she had disturbed the family. She could have a bath any time she chose. One at half past three in the morning was unusual, but she would tell anybody who tapped on the door, 'I couldn't sleep, I'm fine,' and she smiled,

soaking in the warm scented water, hugging herself and
her secret.

It was a lovely secret for a while. It was always a
secret. At least, she told nobody, and she didn't believe
Martin did, because no whisper of that night ever
reached her. All the day she went about filled with
wonderment and singing joy. She was on a high of
happiness, and all evening she sat with Aunt Helena
and waited for the phone to ring. It did a couple of
times, but neither was Martin, and Aunt Helena
stitched away and Lacey sat up until after midnight,
pretending she wanted to watch a very old late movie.

He didn't phone. It was easy enough to find excuses
that first night, but not so easy next day. By the third
night she could hardly bear to answer the phone
because the disappointment was so acute when
somebody else spoke. Aunt Helena was helping to
arrange a W.I. sale of work, friends were phoning about
it, so she was answering the phone that night, and every
time she got up and went into the hall Lacey sat staring
at that damnable bird of paradise on the tapestry
frame, with its sharp black eyes and sharp claws. She
felt as though the talons were digging into her heart.

Denice Watson—as she was then—had told Lacey
how she had waited for Martin Jackson to phone; and
Lacey had felt sorry for her and irritated at the same
time. Now she was doing it herself, and by the end of
the week she knew that he had nothing to say to her.

The holidays ended and she began her final year at
art school, but for a long time she looked through the
post each morning for writing she didn't recognise on
an envelope. Sometimes she got letters like that, or
typewritten, but they were never from Martin. From
him there were no letters, no phone calls, not even a
Christmas card.

The house sold quickly and he didn't come back to
Chadsford for Christmas. So far as Lacey knew he
never came back, although he kept in touch with some

of his old friends. She heard about him from folk who had no idea what had happened that last night, and after a while he began appearing on T.V. news programmes. He was good. He made an immediate impact and went on getting better. He was as successful in his career as in everything else, and Lacey forgot that night.

She hardly thought about him. She had disliked him for years, and nothing had happened to change that opinion. She never wanted to meet him again. Her life was pleasantly unspectacular. She had her Arts Centre and two men loved her, her father and Paul, and that was plenty to be thankful for. Martin would never have put himself out to see her again, but the festival had brought him here, and now he was trying to blow her peaceful life into smithereens for no reason but devilment.

She turned on the light at last and saw her pale reflection in the mirror. 'You haven't changed,' he'd said, 'not by a hair's breadth,' but of course she had changed in five years. In hundreds and hundreds of days and nights. Did he maybe think they could pretend he hadn't gone away the next day, but had stayed around instead, and their relationship could proceed from there?

Except of course that it was the thrill of chase and capture he wanted, not a relationship. He was after her, but he wasn't getting her. Her lipstick was smudged and some of the friends they'd passed coming back from the fair must have noticed that, and those who didn't know she had been stuck in the big wheel with Martin would be hearing about it very soon, and she had to play that down to Paul, to everybody.

Tomorrow was going to be a difficult day. Lacey took a bath and went to bed, and even when she knew that all the music had stopped she could still hear the blare of the fair pounding away in her head ...

She needed an extra dab of blusher next morning and

a lighter foundation to hide the shadows under her eyes. She looked all right then. She didn't look as though she had had bad dreams and she couldn't have said for sure that she had. She couldn't remember any details, but she had an impression of having tossed through a restless and frightening night.

She gave her father his breakfast. He was still in his dressing gown leafing through the Sunday papers, and she didn't have time to start explaining to him. He would be annoyed, after what he had told her about Martin, but later she would sit down and reason that all she had done was meet Martin at the fair and go on one of the rides with him. Surely that was no big scene.

'Pleasant evening?' asked her father, reaching a hand for his coffee cup which was always placed in the same spot but not looking up from his paper.

'Interesting,' she said. He wasn't listening. He murmured, 'Good, good,' and she thought he might well have said, 'Good,' if she had replied, 'They got the wheel going again in the nick of time, I was being seduced up there.'

Things were beginning to stir. It was another lovely day. Shopkeepers were setting up their pavement displays and a few holidaymakers were strolling around. She called at Mrs Bowden's wool shop before she went down to the centre, to collect Jet. The dog was something she could rely on. He wouldn't need placating about last night, as she would probably have to get round Paul. Paul had been disapproving enough about her dancing in the square. When he heard she had made an even bigger spectacle of herself with Martin Jackson—and Charlie Rilke had taken a photograph *and* got a quote—Paul could retreat into a huff for the rest of the week. He mustn't, Lacey needed him; but she would fetch Jet and be sure of one approving admirer for the day.

There was no barking when she knocked on the back door, which Mrs Bowden opened right away, with one blue curler nestling in her fluffy grey curls. 'Young Martin's taken him,' said Mrs Bowden, smiling as though that was fine. 'He said he was collecting him for you.'

'Well, I didn't ask——' Lacey began. Then she smiled herself. 'All right, thanks. By the way, do you know you've still got one curler in?'

Mrs Bowden clapped a hand to the top of her head. 'I pulled them out in a hurry when I looked through the curtain and saw it was a man. Ooh, I could have gone into the shop like that!' She sounded as though that would have been as shocking as appearing behind the counter topless, and Lacey said, 'I'll bring him back later.'

'Who?' asked Mrs Bowden, bright-eyed.

'Jet.'

Mrs Bowden gave a little chuckle. 'Oh, I thought you meant Martin. He's a nice young man. We had a cup of tea together. I told him I always watch him, I think he's very brave.' She sobered and shook her head. 'He goes to some dangerous places, doesn't he?'

'It's his job,' said Lacey. 'He can handle it.' I hope, she thought, although he was no concern of hers; and she had *not* asked him to fetch Jet, and this meant he was either waiting for her or would be turning up at the Centre very soon. It was too early in the day to start fencing with him. She hadn't the strength for it yet. She needed an hour or two to make up for her lost sleep.

She went into the Centre by the side door that opened onto the ground floor. Most of her colleagues had arrived, it was nearly nine o'clock, and Martin was in the woodcarving workroom, talking to Anton who made and repaired violins. Martin had a violin in his hands. He was standing just inside the doorway and when Jet gave his joyful bark he looked across at Lacey, said another word or two to Anton and handed back the violin, carefully as though he was reluctant to let it go. The instrument was beautiful, and Lacey remembered the feel of his hands on her skin and was suddenly shivering.

'Traitor!' she said to Jet. 'Going off with a stranger. Why didn't you wait for me?'

He was an amiable dog but not all that friendly. 'I explained the situation to him,' said Martin.

'Explained it to both of them, did you? To him and Mrs Bowden?'

He would tell Mrs Bowden that he was taking Jet down to the Arts Centre for Lacey. He wouldn't tell her that he was stalking Lacey and Lacey was running from him.

'Of course,' he said, and he smiled as though they were good friends. They were smiling faces around. The tale of the wheel was probably all over the town by now, and she had to treat that as a joke, because it was.

It's up to me, she thought. I know the risks and the price. I would enjoy two weeks of his company, but I know what it would lead to and I would enjoy that too much. Then he would go away and I would have hurt Paul terribly and done myself lasting damage, so it's not on.

He didn't pester her. He didn't really come near her. He was the star attraction around the Centre that morning, because nearly everybody who came in recognised him. He sat while his profile was etched on slate. That brought a crowd of spectators and a queue waiting to have their own portraits done. He helped at various stalls, fetched, carried, and was taken away midday by Mrs Pomeroy, a large booming lady, to give out the prizes at the dog show. 'We didn't know you were staying on,' said Mrs Pomeroy, who was on every Charity Committee in the area. 'But if you are that will be splendid, dear boy. You can be *such* a help.'

Mrs Pomeroy had been a friend of Aunt Helena's, the bird of paradise tapestry hung in her drawing room, and her heart was in the right place, even if she did go at everything like a bulldozer.

'Sure I'll come,' said Martin. He was behind Porteus's and Maisie's stall at the time, next to Lacey's. She had a feeling he was working round to her, and she was glad Mrs Pomeroy wanted him. He smiled across at Lacey. 'Can I take Jet along?'

Jet was on his bed in her corner and Mrs Pomeroy chimed in, 'Splendid idea! He can enter. There's a class for dogs who've never won anything. He's never won anything, has he?'

As Jet was mongrel to the core Lacey considered that was a daft question. 'No,' she said.

'And there's one for the ugliest dog.'

'Do you mind? He stays here. I don't want him getting an inferiority complex,' Lacey laughed, but she didn't want Jet going anywhere with Martin. He was her dog, pretty nearly, and he was staying with her.

'Do you walk him at night?' Martin asked.

'No,' she said.

'Will you?'

'No.'

'See you later, then,' he said, and Mrs Pomeroy and Porteus and Maisie, and quite a few others had listened to that. When Mrs Pomeroy and Martin had gone down the stairs Maisie said, 'I thought you two couldn't stand the sight of each other.'

Lacey shrugged elaborately and said inanely, 'A lot of water's gone under the bridge since then,' because she had to keep this flippant, it had to look like a casual flirtation, which it was to Martin, although to Lacey he was a threat like a circling tiger. 'Actually,' she added, 'I still find him extremely resistible.'

'Tell that to Sunshine!' Porteus guffawed. Paul had just come up the stairs, he must have passed Mrs Pomeroy and Martin, and his expression was not all sunny. It was almost lunchtime and Lacey had intended to phone him, and she was sure somebody had told him about the big wheel.

She said, 'Hello.'

'Hello.' He was very controlled, keeping a stiff upper lip, and Lacey felt her own lips twitching. It wasn't funny, but Paul's expression reminded her of last night in the square when she was trying to get him to dance, and his shoulders had jerked up and down like a marionette's. 'Plenty of folk around,' he said. She was supposed to be colouring another of her outlined sketches, it stood on an easel and she was seated beside it, but she hadn't done much work this morning. Still, she had sold a few pictures, and got an order to copy a photograph.

'Where did you—er—meet up with him last night?' Paul looked across towards the stairs and spoke quietly. He had his back to the next stall. He had moved round so that he blocked Lacey from Porteus and Maisie, but Maisie wasn't missing anything. She was leaning over, neck stretched and ears cocked.

'Walking round the fair,' said Lacey.

'You hadn't arranged to meet him?'

'Of course I hadn't!'

'I don't trust him.'

'So you said. I just bumped into him, and we went on the big wheel—but I'm sure you know all about that. Then I went home.'

'Not on your own.' The tongues *were* wagging. Paul had been told that Martin had been with her.

'Straight home,' she said, 'and as you know, Martin isn't welcome in my home.'

'Are you coming for lunch?' This would go on if she did. Somebody would keep an eye on her stall, but she didn't fancy being interrogated over her ploughman's or pâté. She wasn't hungry as it was, and she told him, 'I'm skipping lunch today, I'm rather busy.'

'Fair enough.' He sounded determined to keep his cool. 'Am I still invited to dinner?'

'Tonight? Oh yes—yes, of course.' That would be another meal for which she would have no appetite, sitting between her father and Paul. 'The usual time.'

He still hesitated, then the words came in a rush, 'I'm sorry, but Charlie Rilke said that when you stepped out of that carriage with Jackson you looked—well—dishevelled.'

Lacey could have murdered Charlie, but she was sorry for Paul. She said, 'So would you have done. That carriage jolted us like mad before it stopped.'

'He didn't try anything?'

She said, 'I should hope not!' shocked at how smoothly the prevarication slipped out, as though she was covering up. She wouldn't have believed that she could look straight at Paul and almost lie to him, even if it was for his own peace of mind.

'He will,' Paul said grimly.

'Then he'll be unlucky. No chance.'

Somebody asked for one of the little sketches hanging on the wall, and Lacey unhitched it and made the sale, during which Paul said goodbye and walked away. When the customer had gone too Maisie was still sitting with her head on one side, eyeing Lacey thoughtfully.

'Come to dinner tonight?' asked Lacey. Two more at table might stop her father, and possibly Paul, from going on about Martin.

'Thanks,' called Porteus from the other end of the stall. He was overweight and Maisie had him on a constant diet, but it didn't do much good as he cheated all the time. Maisie pulled a face and laughed,

'All right, thanks, we'd love to.' After listening to Paul just now she knew the invitation was an S.O.S. She and Porteus had seen Lacey and Martin come out of that carriage at the fair, when Lacey had dashed away through the crowds. They had been joking and teasing in here this morning about her and Martin getting trapped in the big wheel but Lacey hadn't been laughing last night.

'Get up to something, did he?'

'*No!* We fell in a heap and it was quite funny, that's all.'

'If you say so.'

Lacey did say so, and yet Maisie was a real friend. She could have told Maisie, 'Yes, he does fancy me, and I'm scared I could lose my head, because I want him like crazy. But it would spoil everything for Paul and me, so it mustn't happen.'

Maisie would keep her mouth shut, and stay close so that Lacey need never be alone with Martin. Maisie would help her hold him off. So why was she denying, as fervently to Maisie as she had to Paul, that he was any danger?

Unless, in her heart, she was undecided what she was going to do now that Martin had come back.

CHAPTER FOUR

LACEY left the Centre half an hour before closing time. With Porteus and Maisie coming to dinner there would be more preparing to do, and from five o'clock onwards she had been apprehensively waiting for Martin's return.

The Dog Show was over, he would have handed out the prizes by now. There would be old friends to hold him up, fans who wanted to chat, but Lacey felt in her bones that he would be back here as soon as he could, and she didn't want to see him again tonight.

First she had to return Jet to the wool shop. She would have liked to take the dog home with her, smuggle him up to her room, feed him there and talk to him, but if she did her father could break out in one of his animal-allergies, and she was going to have enough trouble with her father as it was.

'All on your own?' asked Mrs Bowden when Lacey handed over Jet. 'Martin Jackson not with you?'

'Why should he be?'

'A little bird's been telling me,' said Mrs Bowden, looking rather like a little bird herself beneath the fluffy grey plumage of her hair, 'that you were at the fair with him last night, stuck in the big wheel.'

'That's right,' said Lacey. 'But today he's helping Mrs Pomeroy with the Dog Show. She suggested we might enter Jet in the Ugliest Dog, but I didn't think so.'

'The very idea!' Mrs Bowden bristled. 'If it's ugly dogs they want that fat old spaniel of hers would take some beating!' Lacey left her simmering, but it wouldn't be so easy to sidetrack her father when he wanted an explanation of her joy-riding with a man who was nearly a murderer in his eyes.

She went round to the back of the house to get in through the kitchen door, and stopped with a gasp of pleasure as she rounded the corner, because there was a great bunch of red roses on the doorstep. They had to be from Paul, a peace offering for last night and today, and it was a lovely way of saying, 'I love you, I trust you.'

She picked them up, inhaling their perfume. I'm so lucky, she thought. We have a good thing going, Paul and I, and I'd be out of my mind to throw it away.

Before she did anything else she attended to the roses. They looked beautifully fresh, but she wanted them to last as long as possible. At least until the fortnight of the festival was over and Martin had gone. Every time she felt stirrings of lust for Martin she would look at Paul's roses and think—these stand for love, and love is for life. She would take a rose with her to the Centre, put it in a single-bloom vase and Paul would see it when he came in. It would be her signal that all was right between them, that even when they were apart she was thinking of him.

She carried them in a Chinese vase into the drawing room, and set them on a low table. The vase was almost translucent, in the palest of greens, with a dripping splash of gold across it and one delicate golden flower. The walls in here were covered in a pale green silken brocade wallpaper, that was old and beautiful and had been here all the years that Lacey remembered. She thought the dark red roses looked breathtaking. She knelt in front of them, taking a final deep breath of their scent, before she went into the kitchen and started peeling potatoes and said, 'Thank you,' to Paul and wondered whether she should try to phone him and thank him right now.

He might be at home, she might get him there. She picked up the hall phone and was beginning to dial when from the top of the stairs her father said, 'Lacey.' He managed to make the two syllables of her name sound as reproachful as a tirade, and she put the phone down. 'Would you come up here?'

His studio upstairs was also his study. The big room, with the big windows facing north, was entirely his domain and he led the way to it now while Lacey followed. She presumed she was about to be taken to task, and she was uncomfortable. At her age she was past the scolding stage, but her father always had the knack of making her feel guilty, if he wasn't getting his own way.

Lacey was on the defensive, starting to explain as soon as she stepped into the room. 'I can guess what this is about, but I can't think why you're making a fuss.'

'I was not aware that I ever made a fuss,' said Laurence Allen, and she was reminded vividly of Paul announcing, 'I do not nag.' Maybe they didn't, but between them they were working on bringing her to heel.'

'But what I cannot comprehend,' her father went on, 'is how you came to be gadding around with Martin Jackson last night when you left here with Paul.'

'I went on to the fair. Paul doesn't like fairs.'

'He shows good taste.' Her father disapproved of anything gaudy and raucous.

'And I met Martin,' she exclaimed. 'And we started talking. I know you dislike him—I used to.' As she heard herself say that her brain clicked. Used to? She still did, you could be physically attracted to a man without liking him, so why had she said 'used to?' 'It was only a fairground ride, for heaven's sake,' she said, 'not a slow boat to China.'

A slow boat anywhere with Martin would be perilous. Even a trip in a rowing boat on a calm lake could end explosively.

'I'm disappointed in you,' said her father. 'You know my opinion of young Jackson, and yet you were alone with him within an hour of what I told you.'

They were not alone, except in that wretched carriage, the fairground and the town were teeming. She said harshly, 'That he killed his father?' That sounded horrific, and she went on quickly, 'Well, I wouldn't know about that, nor why his father should have worried himself to death over Martin, because he's done better than anyone else from round here.'

'Because he's thoroughly selfish. Because he cares about nobody but himself.'

'There's a lot of them about,' she said, and although Laurence Allen would never have applied that description to himself he froze in offended dignity.

'I've said all I'm going to say,' he told Lacey coldly. 'But you've got a fine young man in Paul and I hope you're not going to do anything to upset him.'

He turned away, and she thought of the roses and smiled. Paul shouldn't be upset. Tonight she would be sweet and loving; and sane, because Martin Jackson was a form of madness. She would put on a festive meal, with candles and wine. She had planned blackcurrant tart for a dessert, but instead she would make a mille-feuille. She and Paul would entertain Maisie and Porteus, and her father would see how happy they all were and know that everything was all right.

In the kitchen she set the oven on Mark 8 and took puff pastry from the freezer. She hoped Maisie would forgive the double cream and sugar that Porteus would be shovelling down, he certainly wouldn't settle for cheese and biscuits; and as soon as she could she would have a word with Maisie about Martin.

'Paul's getting twitchy about him,' she'd say, 'and Martin always did have a crazy sense of humour, so if he comes into the Centre again if you could stay right by me I'd be grateful.'

She wouldn't say anything about fancying Martin. She wouldn't even think about that, but if she did that was the word she would use. She 'fancied' him; which was a world removed from the ache and the hunger as if she was starving for him.

Her father didn't come downstairs while she was preparing the meal. Nor while she was laying the table in the dining room, with the silver cutlery and tall pale candles in the silver candlesticks. She took two bottles of wine from his stock. They were replaceable and she would replace them. If he had been down here she would have asked him to do the selecting, but she took something suitable, opened the Mouton Cadet to breathe, placed the Chablis in the fridge to chill, and went upstairs to make herself equally appetising.

It wasn't a party, she wasn't dressing up to the nines, but she put on a blue silk dress with a frilled collar, and dusted silver sparkles on her cheekbones. Paul liked her in this dress, and she dabbed on a little of his perfume and remembered Martin saying, 'It isn't right for you,' and sloshed on so much that the roses wouldn't stand a chance.

She was sitting at the dressing table, hair brushed into shining curls, eyes and lips soft and smiling, until she thought of Martin. As she replaced the perfume bottle in front of the mirror she saw that she was scowling, all softness gone.

It wasn't a pretty sight, Paul wouldn't have recognised her. But it took a moment or two before she could wipe the pugnacious expression off her face, and as she sat back, scolding herself for letting a silly thing like somebody disliking her perfume irritate her, it wasn't soothing to realise that now she was reeking of the stuff she wasn't that crazy about it herself.

She washed her wrists in hot soapy water before she went downstairs. That had been such a waste. Upsetting too, proving Martin could trigger a reaction in her without even being here. He's haunting me, she thought, and she went into the drawing room to look at her roses again and think of Paul.

Her father was sitting in his usual chair sipping a glass of sherry. 'We're expecting company?' he asked.

'Paul and Maisie and Porteus. That's all right, isn't it?'

'Of course. You invite who you like here.' She did. Her father didn't always join them, but she had never had to ask permission. Only now Martin was in town, and he was taboo. Although she was supposed to be cooking those meals for him if the mini-bus fund was going to get its big fat contribution.

'I've cooked a lovely meal, although Maisie's still got Porteus on his diet.' She laughed, launching into an account of Porteus's lapse this afternoon with a bag of doughnuts behind the pottery kiln, when she saw that her father was not amused. He must still be brooding about last night, and her blatant disregard of his wishes. She hoped the evening would thaw him out and she went into the kitchen to deal with the final culinary touches, and stayed there until the doorbell rang.

It was Paul, and Lacey held out both hands to him and threw her arms around him as soon as she had him in the hall. 'Thank you,' she said.

He hugged her back, then asked, 'What for?' He didn't sound as if he was teasing, he sounded as if he was asking, and she murmured, 'This and that,' while her mind whirled. If the roses were from Paul surely he would have brought them with him. She hadn't reasoned like that before, but she did now, and she babbled, 'Maisie and Porteus should be along any minute. Come and have a sherry with my father. You're his very favourite person, which is more than I am!'

Paul followed her into the drawing room, slightly bewildered, and Laurence Allen greeted him affably, ignoring Lacey. No way did Paul acknowledge the roses. It was the time of year for them. Anybody could have picked her a bunch from their garden and left it on her doorstep, although these were superb blooms and she didn't think that was the way it had happened. She knew by now that they hadn't come from Paul, he didn't give them a second glance.

Maisie did. She had looped her long hair high and fastened it with a comb holding a pink silk poppy and she was wearing a pink and purple caftan. Maisie had dressed up, jeans and T-shirts were her usual uniform, but she was here to help Lacey over a sticky patch tonight, what with Paul getting on his high horse and everything.

Lacey let them in, and as soon as they entered the drawing room Maisie sensed the atmosphere. Mr Allen was never what you'd call a jolly man, but tonight he was being very regal, and Maisie's eyes fell on the roses and she gushed, 'Aren't your roses lovely? Oh, I do love roses, they're my favourite flower.' She sniffed them ecstatically. 'Oh, they smell beautiful!'

'I wouldn't know,' said Porteus, and sniffed too. 'I think I've got my hay fever coming on.'

He sneezed to prove it and Laurence Allen shifted back in his chair. He detested other people's ailments. Maisie giggled nervously, 'It isn't catching, but it's going to be a nuisance tomorrow if it doesn't clear up.'

Porteus was the villain in *Sweet Alice*, and although none of the parts called for realistic acting, and Porteus hammed the role to perfection, a heavy head cold would be a nuisance.

'Oh, I don't know,' said Lacey, 'it might make it funnier.' She spoke one of his lines in adenoidal fashion, twirling an imaginary moustache, 'Cub, by proud beauty, the tibe for bock bodesty has passed.'

'I like it,' said Porteus, Maisie went on giggling and Paul grinned. If Porteus couldn't play the part there was an understudy. But Laurence Allen didn't raise a smile, and that was how the evening went.

The meal was delicious; Lyonaise potatoes, sprinkled with parsley, crisp and tender leg of lamb, locally grown peas and cauliflower. The dessert, oozing with cream and blackcurrants, topped with cream and icing sugar, was a party piece.

'I always thought,' mused Maisie, 'that when you lost your sense of smell you lost your sense of taste.'

'Takes different people different ways,' said Porteus cheerfully, gleaming eyes on the mille-feuille,

Porteus and Maisie kept up the conversation, and Paul seemed relaxed and comfortable, and Lacey was her usual bright self. But Mr Allen was very cool. It was something to do with Martin, because when Porteus mentioned Martin Jackson's name Maisie saw Mr Allen's expression. Martin had come into the Centre again just after Lacey left. He was spending the evening at the Pomeroys', and Lacey said gaily, 'Well, he gave out the prizes at the Dog Show and from what I know of Edith Pomeroy she'll have him lined up for half a dozen other jobs over supper.' She laughed, 'By the way, I told Mrs Bowden she'd suggested putting Jet in for the Ugliest Dog and Mrs Bowden said if it was ugly dogs they were after what about fat old Sukey?'

From then the talk took off in other directions, but as soon as she got a quiet moment with Lacey Maisie was going to ask her why Martin Jackson wasn't welcome in this house.

The phone rang just after Lacey had served up the dessert. Her father had declined with a dismissive gesture, 'Too rich for me,' so he had an empty plate before him and Lacey had raised her first forkful to her lips.

He frowned, hearing the ringing, and she got up. She didn't hurry, and she closed the door into the hall quietly behind her.

'How's it going?' asked Martin before she could say a word, although he could easily have been speaking to her father. She would have got here first because she had half expected this call, but he wasn't to know that.

'How's what going?'

'The dinner party.'

Porteus and Maisie must have mentioned that they were coming here. 'It isn't a party.'

'Can I come round for coffee?'

'*No*. Anyhow I thought you were being wined and dined.'

'I made an excuse and left.' She wondered where he was ringing from. The hotel? A callbox? There was a callbox at the bottom of the hill. He could look up at the lights of the house from there, and she could see him in her mind's eye, very plainly, that hard strong sensual face.

'Well, you can't come here,' she said. 'You know what my father thinks about you. And did you leave the roses?'

'Yes.'

'To cause trouble for me with Paul?'

'I never thought about him, actually.' He sounded as if Paul was the last person they should be considering. 'They were an apology.'

'What for?' For not keeping his promise to phone her five years ago? It was a bit late to be harking back to that now.

'For last night,' he said. 'I shouldn't have taken advantage when the wheel stopped turning.'

He smiled when he said 'taken advantage'. Lacey could hear him smiling and she bit her lip because she didn't want him hearing her smile too.

'Too true, you shouldn't,' she agreed.

'So, I'm sorry.'

No, you're not, she thought. You're stalking me, but it won't work. 'How touching,' she said. 'Black Jack says sorry—that's nice. Sleep well.'

She put the phone down and waited with her hand on it for almost a minute, in case it should ring again. But it didn't. Then she went back into the drawing room, where Maisie was refusing Porteus a second helping of pudding. 'Who was it?' her father asked.

'Angela.' Angela was a friend who lived a hundred miles away, and Lacey sat down at the table and picked up her fork again and knew that she was into a conspiracy. From being outgoing and open with nothing to hide, she now had secrets. She drank a little more of her wine, while Maisie told Paul and her father about Porteus and the doughnuts this afternoon. Her father hadn't smiled at that first time round and he wasn't smiling now, although Paul was finding it funny and Porteus didn't care. The joke wasn't on him, he'd eaten two before Maisie caught him.

Lacey had been sparing with her own wine glass while keeping the others filled, and now she was glad that she had. A little more wine and she might not have bothered to fib about the phone call. She could just have told them who it was. She might even have looked straight at her father, who was behaving very badly, and said, 'None of your business.'

When Lacey's father decided to take his coffee upstairs nobody tried to persuade him to stay. In fact Lacey jumped up and said, 'I'll carry it up for you. Your studio or your bedroom?'

'Thank you,' he said, 'but I am still capable of lifting a cup and saucer.' He wished them all goodnight and stalked out, very erect and stiff-backed.

'Was it something I said?' asked Porteus. 'Didn't he want us round here tonight?'

'He's in a mood,' Lacey was sorry about it, but the mood would wear itself out, she was not being blackmailed by it. She laughed and pulled a face. 'Aunt Helena always used to be telling me he's a genius, and geniuses are expected to be moody. Trouble is, she spoiled him rotten.' Tonight Lacey was in no mood to humour him. 'Let's have some music,' she said.

They chose records and sat around and talked while the music played. They were all warmed by the wine and food, but there was a special glow about Lacey. She curled in an armchair, feet tucked beneath her, laughing, arguing, agreeing, as they were all doing. But with an extra edge and sparkle, that made Paul blink behind his spectacles.

She was in good form. Her father was annoyed with her and she didn't seem to care. It could be the wine, but it made Paul say warningly when she reached for her glass,

'I hope you're not going to have a hangover tomorrow.'

'Me too,' she said. 'If the Squire's going down with hay fever all we need is Sweet Alice with a thick head.'

She had drunk less than the rest, but excitement was fizzing in her. She smiled at Paul and picked up her coffee cup instead of the glass, 'Happy now?'

'Good girl,' he said, and again had that uneasy feeling that Lacey was changing in a way that could be beyond his control.

Maisie insisted on helping with the washing up, which Lacey would happily have left till morning. Lacey was still protesting while Maisie was at the sink, donning rubber gloves. Porteus and Paul had also offered, in half-hearted fashion, but when Maisie said, 'It doesn't need four of us,' they did no arguing.

As soon as everything that needed washing up was in the kitchen Maisie wanted to know, 'What was up with your father?' She stacked dripping plates and Lacey began to dry them. 'Was it to do with Martin?'

'He's sulking because I was at the fair with Martin last night,' said Lacey. That was what it amounted to, and it sounded childish.

'I heard you say to Paul about Martin not being welcome here.' Maisie lifted out another plate and turned to watch Lacey's expression, which was wry.

'Yes,' said Lacey, 'well, my father was a friend of Mr Jackson's and he thinks Martin wasn't a good son. Mr Jackson used to come round and tell my father his troubles, and most of his troubles were Martin.'

'What did Martin do?'

Lacey shrugged, 'Search me.' Her father had hinted at heaven-knows-what: 'I know things about that young man nobody else knows.' Specifically there was the fact that Mr Jackson had died poor. Her father blamed Martin for that. Forgery, he had said, forging his father's signature on cheques perhaps, on other things, which would have been mean and wretched and was not Martin's style.

I don't believe it, Lacey decided, picking up another plate. I don't care what Mr Jackson told my father, I don't believe it.

Maisie was saying incredulously, 'Is that all? Most of us don't see eye to eye with our folk all the time. It was a long time ago.'

'Once my father makes up his mind about anything,' said Lacey, 'it takes a lot to shift him. Paul, now— Paul's the apple of his eye. They hit it off from the very first night Paul came here.'

'Well, they would, wouldn't they?' said Maisie. 'Paul always agrees with everything he says.'

So he did, and so usually did Lacey. 'He isn't over-keen on Porteus, is he?' Maisie went on. Porteus was not famed for his tact and there had been occasions when he had ruffled her father's feathers, but Laurence Allen would never have forbidden Porteus the house, nor described him as a 'contamination.' His aversion to Martin Jackson was much stronger, and now that Lacey had gone against his advice and his wishes he was acting as though she had betrayed him.

Well, at twenty-four, maybe it was time she went her own way. Just far enough to assert her independence, her right to think and act for herself. He had done his best to spoil the evening, and she was impatient with him.

'It was a super meal,' said Maisie. 'It was a super evening.'

'Yes, it was.'

'Are you using a new make-up?'

'No.'

'Your skin looks awfully good.' Lacey had a good skin, clear and smooth, but tonight it was luminous, as though she was lit from within. She smiled at the compliment, and wondered if she did look different. She felt different, more alive, and Maisie went on watching her because this was the first time she had heard Lacey say a word against her father, even jokingly. And because she was seeing something in Lacey's smile that looked both reckless and dangerous.

The guests left together, to walk to their homes. Porteus and Paul both kissed Lacey goodnight as she stood at the front door, Porteus in brotherly fashion on the cheek, Paul lingeringly on the lips.

Lacey knew that her own lips were cool, although she returned the pressure, and it was pleasant and reassuring, and she wouldn't compare it with Martin's kiss. She wouldn't think about Martin. ' 'Be, love,' she said, stepping back. 'See you all tomorrow.' Porteus and Maisie would be at the Centre, and she would be seeing Paul during the afternoon for the matinee of *Sweet Alice*.

She watched them go, Porteus and Maisie linked together, making one dark bulky shape, Paul beside them, looking tall and thin. At the gate they all turned to wave and having waved back Lacey came into the house and closed the front door.

As soon as she did she could smell the roses. She had been conscious of them all night, their bright colour catching her eye, the scent of them drifting across like somebody whispering in her ear. She straightened a few cushions in the drawing room, put the records back in their sleeves and closed the music centre, then stood looking at the roses before she turned out the lights.

Of course it wasn't going to work, she was not getting into anything, but she supposed she was enjoying the flattery of the chase. It was flattering, and it was only a game, and she wasn't likely to forget that. She shook her head at the roses and laughed a little.

Light still showed in a glass fanlight over her father's bedroom door, although it was late and he should have been asleep. She thought, I wouldn't put it past him to be asleep and have left this on to make me feel guilty.

She was not going to feel guilty. She was not going to do a thing that would harm him or Paul, and she had a busy day tomorrow while her father could sleep as late as he liked. She went to her room and got ready for bed and slipped between the cool sheets, stretching drowsily. Almost at once she was drifting into slumber, and in her last long conscious breath it seemed to her that she could still smell her roses . . .

She woke clear-headed. So much for the hangover. By the time she was showered and dressed she was charged with energy, like a cornflakes T.V. advertisement. She would have liked to fling the windows wide and sing something silly, then dance down the stairs and waltz round the kitchen and stick a flower in her hair.

Her father sat at the kitchen table, wearing his dressing gown, reading the papers. She was not going to ask if he'd slept well because he would certainly say he hadn't. 'Good morning,' she said.

'Is it?' The sun was streaming in and she felt wonderful and she thought it was a good morning.

'Breakfast?' she offered.

'Please.'

His appetite wasn't being affected. She made his coffee and cooked his breakfast, hearing the mail arrive as she gulped down a quick cup of coffee herself. Lacey always went into the hall and picked up the mail just as Aunt Helena had done. Her father liked his letters put on the table.

He had a couple this morning, which he opened in silence, and there was one for Lacey. The address was typewritten. It was from a girl friend, and she didn't know who until she opened it. Then she looked at the empty envelope and remembered when she had sat, looking at an envelope like this, and prayed it was from Martin. She wouldn't care to live through that private agony again. Not that she would. If there were letters that would be fun, but she was wiser now.

She said, 'I'm off.' Her father said nothing, and she resisted an impulse to repeat it, much louder. Then she relented. 'Look in on the play this afternoon if you've time. It's for a good cause.'

The box office takings were going towards a bed in
the local hospital. Like all the charities it was a good
cause, like the mini-bus. Her father said suddenly,
'When you were with young Jackson did you tell him
you won't be cooking these meals for him?'

There's one down, she thought, wanting to smile, if
you count the brandy snaps. She said, 'No, I didn't.'

'I see.'

It was a stupid thing to argue about, but she couldn't
give way. She said, 'Goodbye, I'm going to be late for
work,' got no answer, and picked up her bag and went,
running round the house and down the drive and
through the gate as though she really was late, although
she wasn't particularly.

She was exhilarated as though she had just escaped
from prison. 'You bought a jail,' Martin had said, 'very
appropriate,' but she ran on winged feet to the jail she
had bought. She wouldn't fetch Jet today, because of
the play this afternoon. If Martin fetched him that was
Martin's lookout.

The front doors of the Arts Centre weren't open yet,
but inside there was activity. Martin was in the
woodcarving room. Lacey looked as she passed and he
looked up from a bench. He was in an olive green T-shirt
and jeans, and seemed completely at home. 'Hi!' he said.

'I didn't know you were into woodcarving.' He was
holding the carving of a dolphin, polishing it with a
linseed-oil rag, and Lacey thought how it might be if he
did work here. Not Martin. Not when the two weeks
were up. But today he could have been one of them.

'Here,' he said, tossing over a wooden egg from a
bowlful, which Lacey caught instinctively. 'Have a
worry egg on me.'

'What have I got to worry about?' She laughed.
'Except Porteus's hay fever.'

'Doesn't he have Maisie to worry about that?'

'He's in the play. He's the wicked squire who chases
me round the stage.'

'Did you shorten your petticoats before you begin? Or he'll catch you.'

'I'm getting it done this morning. I haven't had a chance till now. See you.'

'Of course,' he said. Of course she would see him. Today she was young and it was an intoxicating sensation. She never had been young in the carefree fashion of most girls. If Martin had sent those roses five years ago, this was how the day after the night of the storm would have been.

Porteus, with bleary eyes and a rubicund nose, sat glowering behind his pots, and Maisie asked Lacey, 'Do you think we ought to get Bart Keddy?' Bart owned a tailor's shop and was Porteus's understudy. He wasn't as imposing a figure as Porteus, but he might be an improvement on Porteus with hay fever.

It was a pity. It wasn't a great play, and the acting was barnstorming, but the costumes and the scenery were attractive, and everybody concerned had done a lot of work. And Bart Keddy was on the weedy side for the seducer.

'I'm supposed to be repulsive, aren't I?' growled Porteus, and Maisie sighed. 'Well, I can see why Alice didn't fancy getting too close.' She turned to Lacey again. 'Do you suppose he'll scare the audience away?'

They were giving six performances during the next two weeks and they were hoping tourists would stroll in off the streets. At seventy-five pence a seat for ninety minutes' sit-down it couldn't be bad value.

'They won't see him till they get in,' said Lacey, and went to ask the girl who made patchwork quilts and cushions if she would please turn up a skirt and petticoat on her sewing machine.

The morning passed briskly. Plenty of people wandered in and around, some of them buying. Martin Jackson was the reason some of them came, fans who had heard he was in the Centre, friends who wanted him to talk about old times.

Even when he was out of sight Lacey knew he was here. Even when he was downstairs in the old offices and cells and exercise yard, she knew that he hadn't left the building.

It was as though he was bugged, she thought, with an inward smile, and he couldn't move out of orbit without something in her striking chill. He came up to her stall and sat on a folding stool chatting up the customers. She wasn't expecting Paul. He was at the Little Theatre this morning with the behind-the-scenes team, making sure all was ready for two-thirty this afternoon. But Paul would hear that Martin seemed to have moved into the Centre, and so would her father and so would everybody else, and there was damn-all Lacey could do about that.

He was good for trade, and he had a list of engagements for the rest of the fortnight, thanks to Mrs Pomeroy. He was a celebrity and he was helping the festival for free, and he was a bonus like the sun shining.

Lacey had intended skipping lunch, but Martin went to the nearest pub and brought back a pile of ham and cheese sandwiches, and although she didn't think she could swallow a thing she ate her share. She was beginning to get stage fright. She hadn't acted for ages, not since she left school for art college, and only before friends and neighbours. This time it was the general public and she was starting to quake.

She said softly to Martin, 'I wish I had hay fever—suddenly I'm not looking forward to this.'

'You'll be a sensation,' he told her.

It was all a lark really. If nobody came to see them that would be disappointing, but no more; and if they got good audiences it would be hard to give a bad performance in a melodrama that you were just playing for laughs. 'Remember when the Youth Club did *Pygmalion*?' she said, and he chuckled.

'That's going back!'

'You sat in the audience, and when I saw you

looking bored stiff I dried up.'

'I'm sorry, I didn't know that was my fault.' He remembered it, and he thought she was joking and she was, but now she said,

'So if you're coming to see us please clap and boo in all the right places, and give me a bit of encouragement.'

He leaned to whisper leeringly in her ear, 'I'll encourage you any time,' and she grinned,

'You're trouble.'

'Not me,' he said, but of course he was. Lacey hadn't said thank you for the roses, they hadn't been mentioned this morning. There were always people around watching and listening to even this whispered moment of joking. But she would say thank you some time when they had a little time alone.

They would be alone. She knew Martin would manage that and she would go along with it, but she would go no further than talking. All the same, she felt a flutter of pleasure at the thought, a delicious frisson running through her. Walking and talking with Martin, hands touching, getting to know each other. She would like that very much, and what harm in the world could it do . . .?

She knew her part as Sweet Alice so well she could have recited it backwards. Arrayed as Alice, wearing a wig of flaxen curls, she batted spiky false lashes at the mirror in the women's communal dressing room. There was no change of costume, except for a donning of different aprons, and for the first scene she was the bride of the woodcutter, arriving at her cottage home, wearing a cloak and the expression of simpering stupidity that was the hallmark of Sweet Alice.

The Little Theatre was three quarters' full when Martin took his seat about ten minutes before curtain up, and from then on he was recognised by everybody who came into the hall. He was still signing autographs when the lights were dimmed, and a man with a guitar perched himself on a stool at the side of the stage to provide the background music, a Ballad of Sweet Alice, starting with the inevitable line 'She was Poor but She was Honest.'

Alice fluttered around her new home, twittering her delight, while her husband, also poor but honest, stood around. Sweet Alice's husband was being played by a young farmer called Freddy who had fair hair and a fresh complexion and looked right for his role as a Victorian hero.

The fun started when the wicked squire swaggered in. Everybody booed Porteus on sight, as he twirled his moustache and ogled Alice. His evil designs were rampant from the start. While he was welcoming the new bride of his woodcutter he was eyeing Alice lasciviously and smacking his lips. She just went on twittering, apparently having no idea at all what was going on. Neither had husband William, although he did describe the squire, after Porteus had swaggered off, as a cruel employer who owned the roof over their heads and could throw them out into the snow.

The lights dimmed, and a spotlight came on Alice, wearing an apron to show that a day or two had passed and she was now established in her home. She held a note which she read, from the squire asking her to meet him at the Blasted Oak. 'This is some mistake,' she informed the audience. 'This message is not for me,' with which she tore it into small pieces.

The curtain lowered, and the singer with the guitar went on with the ballad, about the pursuit of Alice by the squire, but she, steadfast in her purity, had so far managed to dodge him. In the meantime, behind the curtain, they were setting up the big scene.

This was the market place; the backcloth was painted as old Chadsford, the stalls had the names of present traders, and it was a cheerful, colourful, bustling scene. Lots of people had a few words to say, there were some comic turns, and through it all the squire was chasing Alice. Every time he reached to grab her she whisked away, and with Porteus sneezing his head off it had the audience laughing.

Finally he cornered her at the pie stand and roared, 'Do you not know that I can ruin your husband?'

'No, no!' cried Alice, bobbing about behind the pies. 'Heaven will protect us. You can do us no harm.'

Oh, but he could. Arrival of husband to whom she fled for reassurance but who had none to give because the squire was threatening him with the sack.

Sweet Alice couldn't believe it. She appealed to heaven again, and then to the audience, and finally, in the idiotic fashion of medodrama heroines, decided she must turn up at the trysting place, creeping out while her husband was sleeping tonight, to appeal to the squire's better nature.

They had thunder and lightning for the last scene—a backcloth of the woods and the great gnarled tree, Porteus gloating and waiting and Alice stumbling in and down on her knees to do her demented act. Her pleas of course fell on deaf ears. The wicked squire had his way—well, nearly—but then the woodcutter arrived with chopper, and the squire got his come-uppance instead.

Alice fainted, down came the curtain, and the ballad singer gave the last verse about the wages of sin, while the audience applauded as though they had enjoyed themselves.

Altogether it was quite a success. There were some empty seats, but most were full, and there were five more performances to go and local bookings for all of them.

'You were terrific!' Paul kissed her soundly as she came off stage. He had watched it all from the wings, and in the changing room spirits were ebullient. Everybody had had a good time, it had gone well, although they did wonder whether Porteus would be over his hay fever by Wednesday. He had been so bleary-eyed in the market scene that he had nearly fallen into several stalls. The girl who was the wife of the understudy said she would warn him, although she didn't think he'd be keen because they all knew he'd never expected to be called on to actually act. All the time people were coming in, the ones who were in the production, the ones who had watched. They were all saying it was great, and Denice said she couldn't remember laughing more.

'Honestly,' she said, 'it was a scream. I thought you were all fantastic.'

Lacey had noticed her in the audience, a few rows back from Martin at first, but she had moved nearer, and when they all took the final bow Denice had been leaning forward in her seat trying to catch his eye. She would have done, of course, as soon as the audience started to leave. For the last ten minutes or so she had probably been talking to him, but she had come in here alone. 'Barry and I are having a get-together tomorrow night,' she told Lacey. 'Just the old gang, they all want to meet Martin again. You will come, won't you?'

Lacey was still removing her stage make-up. She was out of her costume, sitting in front of a mirror in bra and skirt, wig on a wig-stand, eyelashes peeled off, and her face a gooey mess of cream. She wiped a streak away with tonic-drenched cotton wool, and thought, here we go! remembering Denice's hopeless helpless crush on Martin, before he left here, before she married Barry. 'Does Martin know?'

'Of course. You wouldn't be jealous, would you?' said Denice very softly, leaning over Lacey's shoulder and talking to her reflection.

'Hardly,' said Lacey automatically.

There was probably something else she should be doing tomorrow night. She wasn't at all sure she could get along, but of course she wasn't jealous. Just a bit bothered, because Martin had treated Denice coolly while he was here, everyone had known it was a one-sided affair, and when he left for college she had mooned over him until she had only just missed having a nervous breakdown at eighteen. She always sent him a Christmas card; Lacey had seen his card last year to

Denice and Barry. There were several old friends to whom Martin sent Christmas cards, although he had never sent one to Lacey.

Denice shot off to ask another girl who belonged to the 'old gang' if she would come to the get-together, and Lacey went on removing the pink and white mask of Sweet Alice.

The silly story was based on real life, like Maria Marten and the Red Barn it had been dramatised into folklore. It was a tale of jealousy, but Lacey had never been jealous of anyone and it was ridiculous of Denice to suggest that she was.

She was annoyed because she had warned Martin and she could imagine what tomorrow night would be like. A throwback to years ago, with Denice hanging on to Martin. Lacey took another cotton wool pad and her own clear glowing skin emerged. She had been taking her time, but now she worked fast, to get out of this lot and get out.

She *would* go tomorrow night. It was not going to be like it had been years ago, she would see to that. I won't have it, she thought.

Her hair had been pinned flat and she took out the pins, then shook her head and brushed fiercely. She was so angry she might well walk out of here and ask Martin if he wanted to break up Denice's marriage. Lacey had *warned* him. When Denice invited him to her home he should have said——

Well, what should he have done? Say, 'No, I don't want to meet my old friends'? There was nothing he could say but yes, and it wasn't just anger that was seething in Lacey.

She stopped brushing her hair and gulped convulsively. I *am* jealous, she thought. I don't want him to smile at Denice. Or touch her. I don't want him to touch any woman but me. And I must hide that because if he guessed it might amuse him or he might use it. It would be like handing someone a sharp knife and pressing the tip to your heart.

CHAPTER FIVE

LACEY reached for her clothes, stepping into her skirt, buttoning her blouse with shaking fingers. This was jealousy, raw and aching. She felt as vulnerable as a girl starting her first passionate affair—but it should have happened five years ago, while Martin was still a student, before he became a celebrity. It was too late now.

'Will you come?' Denice was asking her. 'You can bring Paul, of course, although really it's only for the old gang.'

We were never a gang, thought Lacey. It was never that cosy. We were just growing up together, living in the same town.

'He's staying for the whole two weeks, isn't he?' Denice's smile was smug.

'Martin?' Of course Denice meant Martin. She just went on smiling, and Lacey shrugged, 'He says so.'

Denice meant to make the best of the two weeks and it was none of Lacey's business, but when she saw Martin again she would warn him again.

Everything had to be cleared away until their next performance on Wednesday afternoon, because the Little Theatre was fully booked all through the festival. Each evening some local group was giving an entertainment. Lacey packed her own theatrical make-up into a box, and was hanging her costume in the cupboard allotted to them when Paul came over to her.

It was still chaos in here. Lacey was the only one changed into everyday clothes and ready to go, and he looked slightly surprised, 'You didn't waste much time,' he remarked.

'I've left Maisie minding my stall as well as her own,'

and she doubted if Porteus was breaking his neck to return to the Centre. Paul had taken the afternoon off to see the launching of his melodrama, but he was on duty and in a hurry now to get back to the Library. He began to tell Lacey again how good she had been as they walked out through the stage door, and she smiled.

'It was fun.'

'See you tonight?' They were parting at the end of the side-street, she had to go down the road towards the old jail, he heading up to the square and the library, and she hesitated. Tonight they had tickets for *The Flying Dutchman* performed by the Chadsford Operatic Society in the town hall. Paul was the opera fan, Lacey could take it or leave it, and she suddenly felt that she could not sit through the crash and clamour of the storm scene.

She asked, 'Would you be mad if I chickened out?' They were going with a group, Paul wouldn't be on his own. 'But I've got a couple of commissions for pictures that I'd like to get done.'

It didn't seem much of an excuse to Paul and he would have said so, but Lacey was moving away, going faster as he watched until she seemed to be almost running through the crowds.

She arrived fairly breathless at the Centre. It was busier than usual, the festival was bringing in the tourists, and Lacey felt a buzz of excitement in the air, as though colours were brighter and more people were smiling.

Maisie smiled as Lacey ran up the stairs and hurried across. 'How did it go, then?' asked Maisie. 'Anyone been signed up for Stratford-on-Avon? Like Porteus for *Lear*?'

'Rudolph more likely,' Lacey grinned, 'with his poor old red nose!' She told them all that *Sweet Alice* had gone like a bomb—well, a cracker, and Maisie had sold several sketches for her during the afternoon so that was good news, and when she saw Martin and Porteus arrive at the top of the stairs together Lacey felt such a rush of affection that it was hard to stay where she was and not dash over to meet them.

Her heart did beat faster when Martin was near. That was silly, but it was an anatomical fact, because she could feel it fluttering away in her rib cage. Like Denice, like all his old friends, this fortnight was going to brighten her life a little. So long as she always remembered how soon it would end, and that it was as much play-acting as *Sweet Alice*.

'Hi!' said Martin.

'Well, hello,' said Lacey. Another thing was the way other sounds faded out. She must watch that, or she might start believing that he was more real than anyone else, that she was attuned to him more than she was to any other man. But she did know when he was in the building and she half believed that she would hear him if he spoke to her in a whisper across this crowded room.

'I'm down for a Country and Western session tonight at the Tavern,' he said. 'Will you come?'

It was the regular Monday group, they were good, but it was some time since Lacey had gone along to listen, because Paul didn't like country music. She wanted to go tonight with Martin, sit at a little table, drink something long and cool, and smile and touch and talk a little. Then walk home, where he would have to leave her at the gate, but even that would be something to smile at.

Only she had just turned down an evening with Paul and it would hurt him to hear that she had gone out with Martin. Blow Paul, she thought, and made a small grimace, then said firmly, 'Sorry, but I must get some work done. I've got some orders.'

'More local scenes?'

'Of course. Do you still want the Grammar School?'

He didn't think much of her as an artist. In the old days, when it was taken for granted that she would go on to art school, Martin seemed to be the only one who didn't think her work was outstanding, and she would demand furiously, 'So what makes you an art critic? Maybe there's something you don't know everything about.'

'I'd still rather have the charcoal burner's hut,' he said now, and she had the craziest feeling that if they went looking for it, over the hills, they would find it as it was five years ago. But she had seen it on Friday night and she must stop this nonsense. 'I told you,' she said, 'it's changed, it's gone. And what about this get-together with the old gang that Denice is planning?'

'What old gang?'

'Your fan club. Denice was always number one fan.' She shouldn't have said that so sharply; it sounded bitchy. 'I suppose you do know all about it?' she said lightly.

'Yes. You've still got a streak of Sweet Alice in your hair.' Martin tilted her chin, holding her face upturned, and rubbed a fingertip along her hairline. It came away with a smear of pinky-white, and she began to talk fast.

'Well, there was rather a crowd in there and I was in a hurry. It wasn't too easy getting greasepaint off. Look at Porteus, he's still got the red nose.'

She couldn't look directly at Porteus on the next stall, because Martin was still holding her chin and rubbing her hairline. But her eyes swivelled evading Martin's eyes.

'This,' boomed Porteus, 'is natural.' He sniffed and sneezed. 'And I could do with a little more appreciation. I suppose the show must go on, but this is ridiculous.'

'You said it,' said Maisie. 'Bart Keddy'll have to take over,' and Martin burst out laughing.

'Bart? Unless he's grown since I saw him last Lacey's bigger than he is.'

'I am not!' yelped Lacey. Martin's fingers were only touching her chin now. He wasn't holding her, and he was rubbing spots here and there on her hairline where the greasepaint lingered. It was the lightest of contacts, but she felt it through and through, and she moved back.

'Thank you,' she said, and got a tissue out of her handbag and began to rub her temples, hard enough to shift anything except the memory of his touch.

After Martin left—with someone else who had known him when he lived here and wanted to talk about all that had happened since—Lacey hung around the stall for a while and then decided to call it a day herself. What she would do, she thought, was get her father a nice meal tonight. She would be in all evening working, and she would like to tell him that the show had gone well. She had never been on bad terms with him before and she wasn't happy about it. Besides, it wasn't necessary. She understood how he felt, but it was a storm in a teacup.

She bought sirloin steak and strawberries which she would marinate in chilled white wine and serve with clotted cream and a dusting of castor sugar. It would be a peace offering, and she let herself into the house and went straight to the kitchen, to unload her basket. She dealt with the strawberries right away, and then started looking around for her father.

He had said nothing this morning about his plans for the day. Nothing much about anything, come to that. She knew that he had festival commitments, but not today, and that he was working on his Academy picture. But he wasn't in his studio, nor downstairs, and she went out into the garden, which was mainly lawns under trees, and there was no sign of him there either.

Then she saw the note on the hall table, an envelope propped up against the telephone reading, 'I shall be out this evening. Back late.'

Perhaps he hadn't known this morning that he would be out tonight. Perhaps he had forgotten to mention it. Perhaps he was still mad at her and didn't want to hear about *Sweet Alice*. He had every right to take himself off wherever he liked and there was really no need to inform the staff, because this was how it had always been. He went his own way and he had never shown any consideration for the women who ran his home.

Aunt Helena had accepted that, and so had Lacey until Martin came back, making her wonder if the life she had was the life she wanted. Now she had all this steak to put in the fridge for another day because there was far too much for one.

She put down the envelope and picked up the phone directory, and found the number of the Cross Keys Hotel and dialled. He probably wouldn't be there yet, but very likely he'd go back before he went out tonight, if it was only for a wash and brush-up.

'May I leave a message for Mr Martin Jackson, please?' she asked, and a weary voice answered, 'Sorry, but he checked out this afternoon.'

'Thank you.' She put down the phone. A lot of people must have been trying to get in touch with Martin, who had found himself other lodgings. A lot of people would offer to put him up, and she wondered where he was. If she had met him tonight he would have told her, but she mustn't go out on the town after she had told Paul she was working.

She had been going to ask Martin to phone her, and when he did she had been going to suggest he came up here for his dinner, which would have meant she only had two more meals to go. If she phoned Paul she would get him. But then he would want her to spend the rest of the evening with him, and he would nag if she went on refusing. She could only think of one companion who would really appreciate the food and then let her get on with her work. She went down to the wool shop and collected Jet.

Bringing him into the kitchen was an act of defiance, as he was forbidden the house. Like Martin. Her father seemed to consider they were both mad dogs. But tonight her father would be back late and Lacey was darned if she was eating alone.

Jet couldn't believe his luck. He scoured his dish in a matter of seconds, then sat and drooled until he was fed with most of Lacey's helping too. She dropped a strawberry on his plate and the wine went up his nose, and he decided it was inedible and biting back, so he curled up on the rug and went to sleep.

Lacey ate the strawberries herself, spooning up the wine, which was now a delicate and delicious shade of pink, and thought it would have been nice if Martin could have come. She could picture him, sitting at the kitchen table, and she held imaginary conversations with him in her head. Just easy talk as though they were easy together.

After she had cleared away the meal she started on her watercolours. The kitchen table was big, with a scrubbed top. She sometimes worked in here and sometimes in her bedroom, but mostly down at the Centre. She liked being with the others and now Jet was company, and his well-fed snores were a comforting background.

She had brought up a photograph to copy into a picture of a house, which the parents were leaving for a labour-saving flat now that the children had grown up and gone. The mother wanted the painting to hang on a wall in her new home, and Lacey copied carefully, catching each detail. New owners could alter even the outside out of recognition, but this picture would keep it as it was now. As long as she lived the woman would have her old home right there with all its memories.

I wish I'd sketched the charcoal burner's hut, thought Lacey. She couldn't have done that, any more than she could have gone back to it, when day followed day with no word from Martin. But now she closed her eyes and she knew how it was, and she started on an outline. The colours would be dark, because it was night, and whether she would try to show storm or just stillness she didn't know yet.

When the phone rang she went to answer it, leaving the kitchen door open, and when it was Martin she had to get her breath because it caught in her throat. 'You're too late,' she would say, as soon as she had her breath back. 'Jet and I have eaten the steak. I tried to get you to ask you to come up for one of these meals I owe you.'

She could hear music faintly in the background. 'Will you come?' he asked.

She didn't see how she could. 'I was supposed to be going to the opera and I called that off because I wanted to finish this picture, so I can hardly——'

'I've got a full schedule tomorrow.' She knew that Mrs Pomeroy was spreading him around. 'If I don't get into the Centre shall I see you tomorrow night?'

'At Denice's? Oh, I'll be there.' She was pleased he was making sure because it meant he wasn't getting involved with Denice. 'I wouldn't miss it for the world,' she said, and the front door opened and her father walked through the hall, giving her a brief nod as he passed, and she gasped.

'What's happening?' Martin asked.

If she ran she could slam the kitchen door, but the rush and the bang would alarm the dog. Better not to get excited. She said softly, 'My father's back and I've got Jet in the kitchen,' and when Martin chuckled, 'It's not funny! He thinks that dogs bring him out in spots.'

'What does he bring the dogs out in?' He was still laughing when she hung up, and at the same time her father shouted,

'Get this brute out of here!'

She did hurry then. Laurence Allen was standing in the doorway of the kitchen, and just inside Jet was bristling to twice his normal size with every tooth bared. Lacey got herself between them and began to calm the dog down, stroking him gently, saying soothingly, 'It's all right, it's all right, it's a friend.'

That was a laugh, and a lie. Anyone would have thought she had filled the house with villains from the way her father was carrying on, keeping well behind her all the time. In twenty-four years Lacey couldn't remember him even losing his temper, but since the festival opened he had seemed to be in a permanent state of simmering anger.

She knew he disliked animals, she wouldn't have

brought the dog in if she had known he was coming back, but his allergy was in the mind. He didn't come out in spots, he just talked about them. 'Oh, do stop making such a fuss,' she pleaded. 'I'll put him in the garage.'

'The dog's rabid!' Jet was still rolling a basilisk eye, his upper lip curled back. The dislike between man and beast was mutual.

'I shouldn't think so,' said Lacey. 'No, of course he doesn't have rabies.' She gripped the collar firmly and her father demanded,

'Who else is here?'

He meant Martin, and Martin could have been. But then he looked at her work, spread out on the table, and thought that meant she was alone. 'I came back for a book,' he said. 'Get that dog back to its owner!' He was white about the jowls, looking at his daughter as if he disliked her almost as much as the dog.

She would take Jet home, later. When the front door closed she loosed her hold on his collar and sat down. There's not much we have in common, she thought. my father and I; and it saddened her.

Aunt Helena had been content to stitch her life away trying to please him, and Lacey's pictures were like Helena Allen's tapestries, attractive and skilful but not great works of art.

Since she had hit on the idea of opening an arts centre with her legacy Lacey had discovered where her talents lay. She was a good business woman, she could organise. She enjoyed running the Centre quite as much as she enjoyed painting her little pictures. In business she might have moved on to bigger things.

Perhaps she wasn't an artist after all, and she wondered what Martin would say if she admitted it. Five years ago she would have told him. But when he went away and never contacted her she had turned back to safety and security. She had never again risked taking chances and getting hurt, although now she knew that he could have been the only man she ever wanted.

She put aside the sketch of the charcoal burner's hut. She might finish that some time, but she shouldn't be rekindling those memories while Martin was still around, because she did not want an affair. As she kept telling herself, it would be madness.

She made a good job of the painting of the house. She was pleased with it and she thought the customer would be. Then she set off to take Jet home, changing her mind as she went out of the garage by the side gate and taking him for a walk instead. He would sleep in the garage tonight and go to the Centre with her tomorrow, then she would return him to Mrs Bowden, because tomorrow night was the get-together at Denice's.

She walked the dog round the outskirts of town and found herself near the Tavern. She hadn't set off to go there, but somehow this was where she had ended up. It was nearly half past ten, the town was emptying. The fairground music had stopped, but you could hear Country and Western rising from the basement, and all the lights in the Tavern were still on and Martin would be down there.

Lacey paused under a lamp-post and asked Jet, 'Shall we go in?' He would be all right. He was a well-behaved dog. She could take him anywhere, except her home. But when a small crowd came spilling out of the pub doors on to the pavement she instinctively turned away. She didn't wait to see if Martin was among them before she slipped into the shadows and hurried to the first turning and out of their sight.

Anyhow, it was too late to be looking for him now. She had better get back and bed Jet down before her father turned up again and there was another row.

She walked quickly the way she had come through the back lane and the side gate, put Jet in the garage, and went into the kitchen to heat some milk.

As she watched the milk rise in the saucepan she thought, I don't want any cocoa. What am I doing, dithering like this? I really wanted to hang around there until Martin came out, but instead I turned and ran. I don't know whether I'm coming or going, and this is a crazy state to be getting into.

She turned off the gas and moved back the saucepan, then started talking to herself, much as she had talked to Jet in the kitchen a couple of hours before, along the lines of, 'It's all right, quieten down, steady now!' Because she was as sure as could be that Martin was not getting confused over her. Wherever he was he would know exactly what he was doing.

Next day Lacey told herself that she was calm and collected again. She took Jet and last night's work down to the Centre, and the woman who had brought the photograph called in and was thrilled to find it ready so soon and looking exactly as she had hoped.

The morning passed rather slowly. Lacey half expected to see Martin, although she knew he was booked for morning, midday, and afternoon fixtures. She was busy herself, upstairs and downstairs, and in the little open-air market that had been the exercise yard. All morning she was restless, although she would never have admitted it was because she was hoping so badly that Martin would come that she couldn't sit still.

He didn't come, but Paul turned up at lunch time, and queried, 'No Martin Jackson?'

'Not this morning,' Lacey said cheerfully.

'Coming to lunch?'

'All right.' This was her lunch-hour and they usually had lunch together. As they went down the stone staircase with the wrought-iron balustrade, Jet at Lacey's heels, Paul asked, 'Finish your work last night?'

'I did one picture. She came in this morning to see if I'd started, and the Lord be praised, she liked it.'

'Were you by yourself?'

He was on the same track as her father, wondering if Martin had been with her, and she asked, 'Are we counting the dog? If we're not I was by myself.'

'Uh-huh,' said Paul.

'In the kitchen, at home.' They came out into the street, and Lacey smiled at a passer-by who was smiling at her. 'Martin was at the Tavern I believe, although I can't personally vouch for that.'

'Not after nine o'clock,' said Paul.

It would be noted when Martin Jackson arrived and left, and she said tartly, 'Whoever told you that should have followed him and then they could have told you where he went.'

'I'm sorry,' Paul said stiffly, 'but there's gossip going on.'

'When isn't there,' she shrugged, 'about somebody or other? Are we eating, or have you brought me out here to cross-question me?'

Lacey couldn't feel indignant, she *had* been looking for Martin last night, and she wondered where he had gone after nine oclock. Probably to the house where he was staying now, and whose was that?

Paul was mumbling and she didn't think he believed her, but she didn't really care. They reached their usual eating place. 'Ploughman's or pâté?' Paul asked as they walked into the crowded bar.

'Shepherd's pie,' she said, for no reason except that she felt like a change. When he went across to order she walked through to the gardens, seating herself on the grass under the mulberry tree. There were plenty of customers out here too. Children came over to ask if they could pat Jet, and Lacey said yes. But she kept the dog beside her because everybody was eating al-fresco and Jet would have thought nothing of clearing the plates that were lying around.

After a while Paul brought out a tray and Lacey said brightly, 'Well, we're being lucky with the weather.' The sun was still shining, but Paul was not relaxing. He had heard that Martin Jackson had been with Lacey at the Centre all yesterday morning. Last night she had called off her date with Paul, and Jackson had cleared off at nine o'clock, and Paul suspected a meeting.

Lacey said suddenly, 'Maisie's dosing Porteus, but he's still snuffling. I don't know whether it's hay fever or a kingsize head cold. Are we getting Bart to stand by?'

Porteus's understudy ran an outfitting shop and taking time off would not be easy for him, and Paul shrugged, 'I wouldn't know.' His mind was not on *Sweet Alice*. Every time anyone came into the gardens he glared across at them, and Lacey thought, he's waiting for Martin to turn up. He thinks Martin's following me around.

She could deny that, but if Martin did call in at the Centre and they did tell him where she might be, he might come, and for the life of her she couldn't avoid a few surreptitious glances herself; so that in the end they were both paying more attention to strangers than to each other.

It was an almost silent lunch. Usually they chatted, but today there was definite restraint on Paul's part. Lacey sensed that it wouldn't have taken much to bring on a scene, in which Paul would have been quiet but very reproachful, and she ate her pie quickly.

'I'm going to Denice's tonight,' she told him. 'Do you want to come?'

'No, thank you.' She wondered if he knew that it was a party for Martin, and while she was deciding whether or not to tell him he asked,

'How's your father?'.

'Still not talking to me much,' she said. 'I don't think festivals suit him.'

Breakfast had been as quiet as lunch. Her father had looked as hard done by as Paul, leaving no doubt that Lacey was disappointing him, and Lacey had reacted the same way then as now. She had hurried off.

Paul was only half through his meal when she stood

up and said, 'If you change your mind about tonight I'll see you at Barry and Denice's around eight.' If she stayed any longer he would be demanding promises she couldn't give. Not right now, when her mind was in such turmoil.

He put down his plate and was starting to say something, but she backed away, calling her goodbyes. As she hurried over the grass, to get round to the road, Jet trotted beside her smacking his lips and she realised that he had probably helped himself to Paul's pâté.

Her father was out that evening and she left a supper tray for him. Then she started to get ready for the party. Lacey had always led a fairly full social life, she had always been a popular girl, but for the past two years most of her invitations had included Paul. Folk round here expected to see them together and although, as Denice had pointed out, he was not one of the 'old gang', they would be surprised if he didn't arrive with Lacey.

He might turn up. Lacey could have persuaded him. Just as she could placate her father by promising to avoid Martin like the plague all the while he was here. That would make things easier at home. Aunt Helena would be turning in her grave if she had any inkling of the present atmosphere in this house. She would be reading Lacey the riot act, about the importance of her father's work and the honour of being his daughter.

Just as she had done five years ago. Lacey examined her face in the mirror of her dressing table, trying to take an impersonal view and wondered how much it had changed.

Not nearly as much as Martin has she thought, although when he smiled he looked younger. Her first sight of him on Saturday morning had shocked her, the lines in his face had seemed so deep, and perhaps she was imagining that he looked younger now.

She had chosen a bright red dress in a soft supple

material that looked like silk. It fitted smoothly over her breasts and was clinched in at the waist with a narrow belt, and the skirt swirled attractively when she did. She had quite a quantity of hand-made jewellery and she decked herself in chains and bangles because she intended to stand out at this party. She could well be the life and soul of it. She was really looking forward to tonight. She couldn't remember having a date that had given her such a thrill of anticipation.

She was walking to the bungalow, it wasn't far, and she was just leaving when the phone rang. She stood, undecided whether to answer. If it was Paul she would have to urge, 'Do come,' because that would be why he was phoning, and she wasn't sure that she wanted him at the party. But a ringing phone is irresistible and she picked it up, and got a girl friend who phoned on average every six months and then talked for ages non-stop about herself.

'You and your father all right?' Lacey was asked at the end of that.

'Oh, fine,' said Lacey.

'You still with Paul?'

'Well, yes.'

'When are you getting married?'

'Oh, I don't know.' I don't know thought Lacey, whether it would be fair or possible; and she ended the call as fast as she civilly could because it was making her late for her date.

She passed the old Jackson house on her way, and looked across almost expecting Martin to walk out of the front door.

There were cars outside the bungalow that she recognised, all local, so Martin wasn't here. She wondered what car he had now. In the old days it was always an old banger that most of the girls in town but Lacey had ridden in. But she could ride in his car now. She knew that, and that maybe she would.

The front door was ajar and the party was in full

swing. Old friends filled the hall, with Barry the host spooning punch into glasses from a Victorian wash-basin on the hall table. Lacey was surrounded and welcomed and asked where Paul was. But everyone who asked looked knowing, as if they guessed why she hadn't brought him.

The door to the main room was wedged wide and from it french windows opened on to a patio and a lawn. Martin stood by the fireplace, with a crowd around him, and Lacey felt the time-warp again. This was like parties in the old days when they had mutual friends but no time for each other. When she walked into a room where Martin was she had always been keenly conscious of him. Antagonism had kindled inside her, so that the sharp words rose to her lips. She had had to clash with him, although she had known she could never cut him down. Always, in those days, Black Jack dominated and the boy she was with dwindled into the crowd.

Well, she thought with humour, he's still the giant around, making the other men seem insignificant, so perhaps it's as well I didn't bring Paul; and beside her Denice gloated, 'We've persuaded him to stay with us!'

Lacey gripped her glass so hard that it was a wonder it didn't shatter. Then she managed to say, tight-lipped but cool, 'Have you now?' as she headed for Martin.

He was coming towards her. They met in the middle of the room, watched by everybody in the room, and he smiled down at her. 'Had a good day?' she asked.

'Yes. You?'

'Peddling my pictures.'

'Did your father come out in spots?'

'If he did he's keeping quiet about them. There's a chill in my home at the moment.' She hissed so softly that the music playing probably drowned her words from the rest, 'I want to talk to you,' and Martin's expression was suddenly inscrutable. His Aztec chief look.

He took her hand, turning her in a swaying step, and they danced, more or less towards the windows and the open air. Others were dancing all around them. Martin moved as she knew he would, with perfect co-ordination, lithe, athletic, sensuous, and she tried to keep from touching him because she was so mad she could have spat at him.

'Well?' he said, when they had traversed the patio and skirted the lawn and reached a far corner of the garden, and then she did almost spit,

'What the hell are you playing at?'

'Who's says I'm playing?' They weren't dancing any more. They were standing, facing each other. 'And what the hell are we talking about?' he added.

'You can't sleep here.' She still had to keep her voice down, so she spoke right into his face as if they were rowing and of course they were. 'Denice has just told me you're staying at the bungalow, and that's a stupid thing to do, because you know what you'd be stirring up. If you're after free lodgings there are dozens of places you could stay. Unless of course, you *are* lusting after Denice, and after what you said about her——'

'I'm staying with the Pomeroys,' he said.

She had been blazing. She would have gone on arguing furiously, for as long as it took to make him listen to her, but that stopped her in mid-flow. 'Oh,' she said in a very small voice, and then she smiled. 'Oh,' she said again. 'Good.'

'I always did have a soft spot for Edith,' he informed her gravely.

'Me too.' When Denice had said they had persuaded him she had meant she was working on it, and it wasn't going to work, and Lacey was so relieved.

'Now if you were to offer me a bed——' he leered and she laughed,

'If Jet brings my father out in a rash have you any idea what you'd do?'

'A fair idea.' She thought there was a hint of

grimness in his smile, and she might have tried to explain why her father had this mighty prejudice against him, 'He thought a lot of your father and he's big on the filial thing, and he doesn't think you were an over-dutiful son.' But Denice had tracked them down, saying as she had at the church fête, 'We can't have Lacey monopolising you like this.' She caught at Martin's sleeve and pouted at Lacey, 'This isn't like the old times at all.'

'Think not?' said Martin, and Lacey blushed pink, and the smiling look they exchanged had Denice goggling.

Lacey enjoyed the party. Martin and she stayed together and she filled him a plate from the buffet and handed it over saying, 'That's the second meal. Only two more to go.'

'The next two,' he said, 'are going to be different,' and that was fair enough, she had cheated shamelessly so far.

Maisie and Porteus had come, although Porteus with his streaming cold was sitting outside on the patio with a glass of whisky and ginger ale, being given a wide berth by most of the others. Bart, the possible understudy, was looking worried. Porteus was usually the picture of health. Bart hadn't expected this, and he spent most of the evening telling anyone who would listen that he didn't have the build or the memory for the part.

After a few drinks he cornered the producer and told her he was not available. She was losing patience. Doreen Richards, a tall bony brunette, was the drama teacher at the local comprehensive. It took a lot to faze her, but now Porteus was losing his voice and Bart had certainly lost his nerve, and she had had several glasses of punch herself and she shrieked, 'What am I supposed to do? It's too late for anyone else to learn the part. Why did you agree to understudy if you never intended to get up there and act if you had to?'

There was a hush, the shriek was piercing, and then Martin said, 'I'll do it.'

The hush lasted, and Doreen said as if she could hardly believe her ears, 'You will?' rushing on without waiting for confirmation, 'But that would be absolutely super! They'd come to see you. We could put your picture up outside, that would fetch them in. Well, yesterday afternoon the audience were paying more attention to you than they were to the play. You could learn it, couldn't you? You could ad lib if you couldn't remember it all.'

'Give me the script,' said Martin, and Bart offered to go home and fetch his right away.

It seemed the ideal solution. Everyone could see that there would be full houses if Martin Jackson was in the production, and Lacey wondered why she hadn't thought of it before. He'd learn his part in no time, that would be no trouble to him, although they wouldn't be able to get in a rehearsal. 'No problem,' he said when she mentioned that. 'I'll come round to the Centre in the morning and you and Porteus can cue me.'

'You're on,' said Lacey. 'Although you should have a moustache to twirl. As you don't you'll have to sneer a lot, and maybe somebody can lend you some riding boots.'

Paul's seemed to be the only unenthusiastic voice. Next day he rang Lacey at the Centre mid-morning. He had been told as soon as he got into work that Martin Jackson was playing the villain in his melodrama, but this was the first chance he had had to get to the telephone and he didn't know whether to blame Porteus or Bart. He wanted to blame somebody. They were all acting as though Roger Moore had joined the cast, but Paul would have preferred Porteus to carry on croaking rather than have Martin Jackson take on his role.

'What's he doing it for?' Paul asked Lacey, and she said,

'Charity.'

Of course it was for charity, but it meant Jackson spending more time with Lacey, and Paul was far from happy about that.

'Is he any good at acting?' he demanded, and Lacey said.

'But this isn't acting. This is just for laughs. Shall you come round this afternoon and see us?'

'I can't take time off again,' said Paul. 'I'm short-staffed,' and he hung up, and he wasn't laughing.

Martin knew his part. He was rattling it off, word-perfect, behind the pottery stall, with Porteus and Maisie checking him, when Lacey went back from her phone call and said, 'Paul wants to know if you've had any acting experience. Perhaps you should have auditioned.'

She was in a giggly mood. She wondered if the news of the cast change had reached her father and if he would be in the audience. But even he could hardly object to a sure-fire way of filling the Little Theatre. People were going to pay seventy-five pence to see Martin Jackson playing the villain, and if he appeared for the rest of the run perhaps they could raise seat prices to a pound.

Martin's picture was up outside the theatre. A photograph from a poster announcing the opening had been superimposed on a big white sheet and scarlet letters proclaimed APPEARING HERE ... MARTIN JACKSON in THE TALE OF SWEET ALICE, OR MURDER UNDER THE BLASTED OAK ... Seats 75p.

A queue was forming by the time the cast started arriving, and Doreen was organising advanced bookings for Friday. In the dressing room where Lacey changed into her costume everybody was high with excitement because this was like winning the jackpot. This could be the top money-spinner of the festival, and House Full had gone up well before the curtain was due to rise. The guitar player who sang the Ballad went out and sat on his high stool and strummed and sang to the packed audience, who were getting a concert as well for their money.

Lacey put on her pink and white face, with all the girls around her chattering and laughing, turning themselves into Victorian market folk and housewives; and at two o'clock she stood in the wings with 'William' to go on stage and open the play as Alice, the bride, entering her cottage home.

Alice and William delivered their opening lines while the audience waited for the villain to appear. On Monday Porteus had strutted in and the audience had booed and it had been fun, but when Martin strode on to the stage they were quiet. He was in riding boots, breeches, open-necked shirt, and he looked handsome as Heathcliff, and somehow in that moment the mood of the play shifted and Lacey's pulse took on a quicker beat.

The rapport between her and Martin transcended their stilted speeches. Alice was not supposed to know that the squire was watching her, but as she moved around the stage she watched him, sometimes from under lowered lashes, sometimes directly, as if she couldn't break the eye contact. It was holding her. She was caught. Martin did none of Porteus's leering, but the scene was electric, you could have heard a pin drop. And Lacey was playing Alice differently, saying the same speeches, but now they were a smoke-screen because she knew that the man who had just walked into her home desired her.

Under the greasepaint her colour was rising, she was breathing faster. Martin hardly moved. Porteus had followed Alice around the stage, but Martin stood, arms folded, saying his lines in the controlled slow-spoken voice the audience had heard on their T.V.s and never taking his eyes from Alice.

When he made his exit she was standing by William. On Monday she had gazed up into William's face while he was making his speech, but today she had turned her head towards the 'door' where Martin was standing in the wings. She felt that Alice would have done that. The sexual pull between this Alice and this squire would have compelled her. Besides which, Lacey was not sure at the moment if she was Alice or Lacey.

This was another play. Two plays: a pasteboard melodrama when Martin was off-stage, and something fiercely erotic when he and Lacey were together. In the market scene where she had dodged Porteus between the stalls, the comedy acts were still laughed at, but Martin and Lacey skirted each other like duellists. The words meant hardly anything. This was highly charged body language, and although they never touched everyone in the audience was waiting with bated breath for when they did.

It didn't happen in the market scene. Lacey came off-stage from that to find most of the cast and the backstage helpers looking bewildered and Doreen literally rubbing her hands with glee. 'This is *much* better,' she chortled. 'After all, it must have been a steamy tale.' She jerked her head towards the audience. 'They can't wait for the seduction scene!'

The ballad singer was filling in while the market scene was changed to the blasted oak by midnight, and Martin, standing by, grinned at Lacey, 'We make a good act, don't we? The chemistry seems to be right.'

'Just remember he gets his head chopped off in the end,' she said. It was a play, an act, and she mustn't let it get under her skin. She took the hooded cloak, and yanked off the mob-cap she had worn for the market scene, and the lights were dimmed for the final act and 'storm music' was switched on.

Thank God the storm wasn't real. It was tinny and phoney. Nothing like the storm when they had sheltered in the charcoal burner's hut, but near enough to bring back memories and while Martin was reciting Porteus's lines she wondered if he remembered.

She pulled up the hood and stumbled on to the stage. She had to plead, go down on her knees, but this Alice didn't kneel. She made her speech with her cloak clutched around her, then she had to go into Martin's arms and get the scene over with, and she went on babbling her part, her voice huskier than ever while he spoke his, 'Why did you not reply to my messages? The time for modesty is over, my proud beauty. You know the price.'

The cloak fell from her as she stepped towards him. As soon as Porteus had hold of Alice William had charged in brandishing his axe and Alice had promptly fainted away. But in the moment she reached Martin he slipped the dress from her shoulder and put his lips to her skin, and every nerve in her responded. If William hadn't bounded in she would have gone up like flame. She had to faint here, she had to fall. She threw herself away, and a gauze screen came down for a shadow show of the murder, while the ballad singer finished the sad saga of Alice Gough.

The audience loved it. They clapped and clapped as the cast took bow after bow, and when the final curtain dropped everybody connected with the production was euphoric. Lacey was the only one who suggested that Porteus might be okay for Friday. 'If he is he won't mind,' said Doreen, which was true. 'You will go on playing it, won't you?' They all stopped talking until Martin said,

'If you want that,' then the babble went on.

Lacey turned towards the changing rooms and Martin was behind her. 'Do you mind if I go on?' he asked, and she shrugged, walking down the corridor.

'Why not? It's for charity. But no bodice ripping next time, if you don't mind. Remember it's a play.'

She was first at the changing room where the door was closed. Martin reached across to open it for her and said, 'The script's the play. The chemistry is real.' He could have seduced her. Right there on the stage, his lips and his touch could have blotted out all those people staring at her. This physical power he had over her was a killer, and no amount of fooling and pretending could change that.

The others were coming. Lacey stepped past him. He would go on down the corridor to the men's changing room. She said, '*This* time I mean it. Leave me alone. Keep away from me!'

Martin looked hard at her for a moment. Then he said quietly and without argument, 'Very well.'

CHAPTER SIX

LACEY believed him. Martin would leave her alone. In that moment he had decided that the game was not worth the candle and he wouldn't trouble her again. She was safe, and she was thankful because she didn't want to be a laughing stock for the rest of her life. Nobody knew what a fool she had made of herself five years ago, but this time the town was talking. If she went overboard again for Martin Jackson they would know, and it would be pathetic.

The others were coming into the changing room now, still chattering about the play and how the takings and advance bookings this afternoon had been nearly as much as they'd hoped to raise in a fortnight.

'You were fantastic,' everybody seemed to be telling Lacey. 'Honestly, I had shivers running up and down my spine! The two of you were just incredible,' said one girl, giggling at the memory, then she asked what they were all wondering, 'Is there anything going on with you and him?'

'No,' said Lacey. '*No.*'

She was going straight round to the library to Paul, before he heard somebody else's version of this production, and again she got off her greasepaint and out of her costume as fast as she could, slipping through the little crowd outside the stage door, who didn't recognise Alice without her blonde wig, and anyway were waiting for Martin.

Lacey wasn't first at the library with the news. The carroty-haired girl, who had tried to dance with Paul on Saturday night, looked up from issuing books and whistled soundlessly as Lacey appeared at the counter.

Out of the corner of her mouth she said, 'They say you're doing Lady Chatterley next week!'

'Is he in?' Lacey asked, and the girl nodded, and watched while Lacey knocked and opened the door of Paul's office.

'Sorry I missed it,' said Paul, who was sitting behind his desk and glaring through his spectacles. 'It seems to have been hot stuff.'

Lacey managed a laugh. 'Well, it ended in murder so perhaps it was. We got a full house anyway and we're almost booked up for Friday.'

Paul didn't say, 'Well done.' He said, 'He's taken on the part for the run, then—and what about Porteus?'

'You know Porteus won't care, and they'll come to see Martin.'

She stood in front of the desk, feeling like a delinquent schoolgirl in the head's study. 'And when are you seeing him again?' Paul demanded, fingers tapping the top of the desk. 'At the Centre this afternoon? Tonight?'

Martin would not visit the Centre again. He wouldn't ring her or come looking for her. It would be like that other time when he had walked away, and she said, 'Next Friday's show, I suppose, but probably not till then.'

Paul frowned, considering that, coming up with, 'You know what they're all saying?'

'Then they're all wrong,' said Lacey wearily.

'What about tonight?' Paul's eyes narrowed even more, he was still suspecting her of secret meetings, and she said,

'Come to my place and have a meal. You can help me make my peace with my father.'

If she was making her peace with her father her little rebellion must be over, so Paul said, 'All right.'

I will have both of you together again, thought Lacey. The two men in my life, who are sure they know best. And maybe they do, because the way I feel about Martin could tear me to pieces.

She was teased, at the Centre, about the play. Some of her colleagues had seen today's matinee and gone back to report that it was a knock-out. Those who hadn't bothered before were all set now to catch a showing before the festival ended.

'What about this striptease in the last act?' Porteus put on an expression of mock shock. 'I didn't find that in the script.'

'It was not a striptease,' said Lacey. 'It was half an inch of shoulder, and Paul will probably be watching on Friday so I think we're cutting it out.'

She joked about it all, and Paul turned up to collect her just after five o'clock, and stayed around her stall until the Centre closed. Anyone who arrived after that saw him, and it seemed to be Lacey and Paul again, and there was no sign of Martin.

Lacey would not have been surprised to find another 'Out tonight' note from her father, but he was home and she was glad she had brought Paul with her. The two men talked in the drawing room while she prepared their meal in the kitchen.

She laid the table and called them to it. She presumed that her father had heard all about *Sweet Alice* this afternoon, although she didn't think he had been in the audience. Nobody had mentioned seeing him. But she was sure he and Paul were discussing it while she was heating up the bortsch and preparing salads and cold meats for the main course.

Her father was looking slighly less grim when they took their places at table, although his first words as he picked up his soup spoon were, 'So now we have the privilege of seeing Martin Jackson performing in Paul's play.'

Now I say sorry, thought Lacey. He wants an apology for the way I've been carrying on, and I don't want to talk about it. I don't want to have to say or hear Martin's name. She sat back in her chair, her fingertips pressing against the table's edge, and said,

'He's a celebrity, people will pay to see him, and I don't want to discuss it. It's nothing to do with me.'

She looked straight at her father, 'I know why you don't like him, and fair enough, you have your reasons; and I know why you don't,' shifting her gaze to Paul. 'But I'm here, feeding you, and this may make your minds easier—after the show this afternoon I asked him to keep away from me because although he obviously wouldn't give a damn about local gossip, you both do and I suppose I do as well. And he said he would. No argument. Happy now? And could we all get on with our meal?'

Her outburst startled them, but then she saw them both relax and it was almost like last week. It was hard to realise that Martin had only been here for five days, but tonight her father was almost his old self, and Paul stayed until midnight. He would have stayed longer if Lacey hadn't looked at him bleary-eyed and yawning, and said, 'Sorry, I've got to call it a day—I'm worn out.' But after Paul had gone it took her hours to get to sleep . . .

There was no sign of Martin in the Centre on Thursday. They were busy, and Lacey painted at her easel behind her stall, and Paul collected her for lunch. They went to a snack bar and discussed all sorts of things without mentioning Martin's name once. They had passed the Little Theatre with his face on the poster and Lacey looked away from it, just as she had before he came. Paul only gave it a quick glance, then he reached for Lacey's hand and tucked it through his arm, and she walked along beside him, feeling out of step although they were both taking the same strides.

As they ate open cheese sandwiches Paul said, 'If I can get Saturday off how about going down to Eastbourne for the weekend?' His parents lived there, and his sister. But they were right in the middle of the festival, and the Centre was open all weekend, and she said, 'We've got the customers coming just now, I might be missing sales.'

'Just a thought,' said Paul.

'As soon as the festival's over,' said Lacey.

Martin was here and there. She heard about him, from friends who watched her when they mentioned that he was looking up old acquaintances, helping with the charities. It was nothing to do with Lacey any more, and she hoped she made that clear. Not in words, but by her casual manner.

Friday was quite a day. Not only another matinee but the morning the *Chadsford Herald* appeared, with its pictures of the opening of the festival. Lacey and Martin, stepping out of the big wheel, had photographed very clearly, and to her eyes Lacey looked as though she was crawling out of a haystack. Beside her Martin seemed quite neat and tidy, and that was mainly because he was smiling and cool while she was still in a state of shock.

The caption mentioned the big wheel breakdown, and here was Martin Jackson, who had opened the festival, with his fellow passenger Lacey Allen, local artist and daughter of Laurence Allen. R.A. '"It was quite a view up there," said Lacey. "We hardly noticed the time passing at all," joked Martin.' Then it went on to say that Martin had taken over Porteus's part in *Sweet Alice* opposite Lacey, proceeds towards a bed in the children's ward of Manor Park Hospital.

That was good publicity for the show, but so many people suggested sticking this picture up outside the Theatre because it should have been a scene from the play, that Lacey thought she would scream. They were all joking, of course. They thought Lacey looked that way because she had just been shaken up and scared by the wheel breaking down, and she hoped they weren't noticing how her lipstick was smudged.

Paul said he'd seen better pictures of her and left it at that, and the girl reporter from the *Mercury* turned up

at the Centre to ask how close a friend was Lacey to
Martin Jackson. 'Not close at all,' Lacey snapped, and
the reporter said that was more or less what Martin had
said and that some of Martin's friends had arrived in
Chadsworth this morning to see the matinee this
afternoon.

They were an eye-catching lot. There were about a
dozen of them, mostly well-known faces, including the
girl who had been going around with Martin recently. It
was the first Lacey had heard of her, she hadn't read
about Martin if she could help it for years, but she
knew the young actress when Maisie mentioned the
T.V. series she appeared in. 'Now you are scaring me,'
said Lacey. 'Real professionals watching!'

Martin's party were found seats in the front row and
Lacey peered through the curtains to see them. The girl
in the centre of the row had hair the colour of bright
copper, curled close to her head. She was laughing up at
Martin, who had his back to the stage, facing his
friends, and Lacey stepped away from her tiny
peephole, quickly, as though she had glimpsed
something terrible. If anyone did let themselves start
caring for Martin Jackson life would be heartbreaking,
filled with girls like Sandra Scott who was so beautiful
that it would be no use at all trying to compete.

Paul arrived at the theatre shortly before curtain up,
and stood watching in the wings as Lacey and William
made their first entrance. When Martin went on today
there wasn't Wednesday's awed silence, because his
friends started the clapping, but it was still a smash hit.
Lacey was very good as Alice. She could act even if she
wasn't professional standard, and although she kept
looking at Paul standing in the wings and reminding
herself that it was all pretence, there was still this
undercurrent of excitement whenever she and Martin
were on stage together.

The applause at the end was as prolonged as on
Wednesday, and when the curtain came down and

Martin's friends came swarming backstage Lacey said to Paul, 'If you could get tomorrow off I think I would like to go to Eastbourne.'

He said he could. She called at the Centre, and explained that she was taking a break. Then she went home and packed a weekend case, then arranged for the woman who had been Aunt Helena's daily for years to look in tomorrow and Sunday to see to Laurence Allen's meals. Her father was in his studio, and Paul had probably phoned him about this, because he said at once, 'Yes, you'd enjoy the break. Why don't you stay on for a few days? You could get a train or a coach back, or perhaps Paul could come down for you next weekend?'

She had work to do in the Centre, and she was acting in the play, but he sounded as though none of that mattered, and probably her activities outside this house did seem unimportant to him. Perhaps they were, but she said, 'I must be here on Monday. We thought we'd drive back early, that gives us all Sunday.'

On the way she told Paul, 'My father says I ought to be staying the week. Nothing like inviting myself for a good long stay, and I don't know who he expects to run my stall.'

'The others would keep an eye on it for you,' said Paul. 'And you know that my folk would like to have you.'

'I can only take the weekend,' she said, but she thought. I would like to stay away until Martin and his girl-friend have left. She guessed that Sandra Scott would be staying on next week. If she did there would be a couple of celebrities loose in Chadsford. Maybe they should ask Sandra if there was any chance of her playing Sweet Alice then it really would be a star-studded cast.

'What are you scowling about?' Paul asked, and she pulled down the vizor and said that the sun was in her eyes.

It was an enjoyable weekend. Paul's father and mother couldn't have been nicer to her, but then they always were nice. They both looked a little like Paul and they always made Lacey feel at home. She had the room she had had on previous visits, right at the other end of the landing from Paul's room. She knew he wouldn't risk any nocturnal trips that might be overheard by either of his parents, and she slept soundly and undisturbed.

The house was near the sea-front, and they spent Saturday being holidaymakers, walking along the promenade looking at the shops, taking in a show at night. They had Sunday lunch at Paul's married sister's, then went down on the beach again, where Jennifer's husband made a sandcastle for his two small boys, Paul read a Sunday paper, and Jennifer lay, glistening with sun-tan oil, on a large striped towel. Lacey had come in from a swim, and flopped down beside Paul, rubbing her hair dry and laughing with the children, who were fat and rather adorable.

'When *are* you two going to get married?' Jenny asked. She was an obsessive matchmaker and she thought Lacey would suit Paul.

'It's up to Lacey,' said Paul. He had said that before too, and he meant it.

Jenny looked well on marriage, Lacey decided, plump and contented, and she felt warm and lazy herself and there had been something dreamlike about the whole weekend. It wouldn't have taken much to make her decide that this was the life for her. Being with Paul and part of this family. Nothing she couldn't handle in the years ahead.

And then she saw the man with the dark curly hair, and it was like being kicked in the stomach. She had the towel over her head, and she glimpsed him out of the corner of her eye, and for a moment she thought it was Martin. It wasn't. This man was darker-skinned and looked like a Spaniard, perhaps on holiday or maybe a waiter from one of the hotels, running towards the sea with a crowd of others. But that first glance had shaken her to the core.

She rubbed her hair harder, all the lazy languor gone,

jolted wide awake, and thought, I couldn't promise to marry Paul while anything that reminds me of Martin does this to me. It was Martin she was seeing now, as vividly as she could see Paul and Jenny. He was so clear in her head that even after the festival finished it was going to take a long time before she was free of him again.

They drove away from Paul's parents' house as dawn was breaking. Quietly, to waken no one, or his mother would have been downstairs, making sure they had had breakfast. Lacey had left two packages behind, tobacco and perfume in their favourite brands and extravagantly large sizes. These were thank-you gifts for a lovely weekend, and perhaps she was apologising—although they wouldn't know it—for not loving their son.

That wasn't entirely true. She did love Paul. If Martin hadn't come back perhaps she would have married Paul, but now he would need too much patience. She couldn't tell him that she still thought he was special but she was burning up for another man. It would burn itself out, she hoped, like a high fever, but she couldn't say how long that would take. Nor for how long she would be convalescent afterwards.

Paul thought she was tired because she looked pale and she was quiet. The radio played, news headlines and music, as they came into Chadsford just before nine o'clock. 'Drop me off at the Centre,' said Lacey. Her case and coat were on the back seat and she reached for them. 'And thank you, and thank them, they are nice.'

She opened her door and put her case on the pavement, and Paul caught her hand and smiled and said, 'I'm glad everything's all right now. See you for lunch?'

'No, I'll probably be running around. I know I'll be rushed off my feet today. See you tomorrow.'

Yes, he said, and the car pulled away from the kerbside, up the hill towards the town square and his flat, and Lacey stood watching it, holding her coat and her little case, wondering how she could ever have imagined that she and Paul were on the same wavelength. How could he believe that everything was all right when she knew that everything was horribly and hopelessly wrong?

Once she stepped inside the Centre she had no time for moping. There was plenty of activity there. Everybody asked if she had had a good weekend and she said of course she had. So had they, they told her—business had been good Saturday and Sunday.

Porteus was throwing pots in the pottery workroom and his voice was booming again. But Lacey must be joking when she asked if he was playing the squire this afternoon.

'The audience would lynch me,' said Porteus cheerfully. 'So would the hospital staff. I don't know who did the fund the biggest favour—me going down with hay fever or Bart losing his bottle.'

Lacey laughed, 'Perhaps they'll put a plaque up to both of you over the bed!'

In the room above Maisie was rearranging the shelves behind her stall and when Lacey ran up the stairs she called across, 'I've got some more orders for you.'

'Lovely,' said Lacey.

'Nice weekend?'

'Lovely,' said Lacey again.

Maisie put down a small black-glazed bowl on the end of the shelf and came from behind her counter to meet Lacey and ask, 'Everything all right?'

'Of course,' said Lacey. Paul thought it was, but with him it had been a statement, not a question. Maisie was unconvinced.

'Funny you taking two days off right in the middle of the festival,' she said, and followed Lacey into the corner of Lacey's stand.

'Yes,' said Lacey quietly. 'Well, maybe I found the festival a bit more than I bargained for.' She stood looking at one of her own pictures on the wall. A local scene, like they all were, this one showed the hill in the background, and she thought of the charcoal burner's hut, and said, 'Maybe I'm beginning to wish I'd never heard about the wretched hiring mops.' Then she turned and smiled brightly.

'Forget that, eh?'

'Sure,' said Maisie. 'Somebody wants to know if you can do that picture of the wishing well in the bigger size. They'll be in towards the end of the week. There's another photograph to copy too.'

'Thank you,' said Lacey.

'Talking of hiring mops,' Maisie went on, 'Martin's paid up.'

So he wasn't holding Lacey to her bargain. She hadn't thought he would, but if she had been asked she would have provided a meal before he went away. She began to busy herself with her display, and it was an hour or two later that she asked, very casually, if Martin's friends had stayed for the weekend.

'Some of them did, I think,' said Maisie, and then a woman decided to buy a big pricey terra-cotta bread vat, so Lacey didn't hear if the copper-haired actress was one of the ones who had stayed, and might still be here. She didn't like to go back to the question, when Maisie had completed the sale, as if it was important to her.

Lacey had shopping to do this morning, food to get in. At about half past twelve she went downstairs with her basket and stopped to ring home before she left the Centre. The phone was in a small room on the ground floor. The walls were covered with posters and there was an old desk, grey filing cabinets, a big iron safe and shelves of reference books. Lacey usually took her own clerical work home, but the rest of them sometimes used this as an office. It was empty at the moment, and she dialled her number and after a while her father answered.

He had been looked after very well, he told her, and

that didn't surprise her because somehow he always was. That was really all they had to say to each other, but she knew that things were back to normal for him. He had beeen reassured by her weekend away with Paul. He would see her this evening. And now she would go off and shop for him and life was already returning to the old routine.

She put down the phone and looked through the window at the exercise yard. The stalls looked gay in the sunshine with customers wandering around. But it wouldn't be many months before it was a winter's scene, and Lacey shivered as if the first snowflake was falling.

The phone rang as she stood there and she picked it up. 'Chadsford Centre of Arts and Crafts, can I help you?'

'Very nice. I bet you had elocution lessons.'

'Martin!' She had to smile.

'Lacey,' he said, and there were only a few more days to go, and she could hardly bang the phone down. She asked, 'And what can we do for you?'

'About those meals.'

'I hear you've paid up.'

'So how about coming and having lunch at the Pomeroys? You could cook the sausages. Then we could go on to the theatre.'

It sounded straightforward enough, but she hesitated. 'Not just you and me?'

'Three of us.' You and me and Sandra? she wondered. 'Edith and you and me,' he said. 'Will she be protection enough, if you feel you might need it?'

'I'd back her against a Sherman tank,' said Lacey.

'Right,' said Martin. 'See you in the kitchen.'

Two minutes later and he would have missed her. If she had gone straight off without phoning home first she would have been out of the Centre when he rang. Coincidences like this were always happening, but there was an element of fate about them. Of course she couldn't admit she was scared of even seeing him, and of course she wasn't. She was going to the Pomeroys. She called at a supermarket on the way to do her shopping, deliberately delaying, but she was being drawn to the big house on the green as surely as though an invisible cord was reeling her in.

Mr Pomeroy was head of the leading law firm in town. The Pomeroys were prosperous, their elegant Edwardian house stood in cherished gardens where the flower beds were a riot of roses and sweet peas on this late July day.

The perfume reached Lacey as she walked up the drive, and as she arrived on the door step the door opened and Mrs Pomeroy, in a grey chiffon hat and a silk suit that rivalled the flower beds for colour, said, 'Come in, dear child. Sorry to be rushing off like this.'

'You're not staying?'

'Another time,' said Mrs Pomeroy. 'Ladies' Circle lunch.' She gave Lacey a smiling appraisal. 'My goodness, you're looking pretty. How's your father?'

'Er—very well, thank you,' said Lacey. Martin was in the hall and as they both watched Mrs Pomeroy, with her fat old spaniel at her heels, walk round to the garage, Lacey began to say, 'You told me——'

'Would you have come if I hadn't?' he said.

'I'm not sure that I would.'

'What do you think I am, a sex maniac?' He was laughing at her, and she grinned too, looking a little shamefaced and feeling an idiot.

'So help me,' he said, 'I'm not. But I thought things between us were getting rather over-dramatised. Don't you agree? I'm not denying the chemistry, but if I'd been the squire Sweet Alice would only have had to say "Shove off" and mean it and there'd never have been a play.'

She laughed again. He couldn't really know how she felt when he was around, and there was no reason why they shouldn't have lunch together. 'I'll cook the sausages,' she said.

'They're almost done.'

'You did them?'

'Not Mrs Pomeroy, in that get-up.' He led the way into the Pomeroy kitchen, which was fitted in old pine, all gleaming in the sunshine. The table was laid for two on a yellow check tablecloth, and Lacey took out some of the delicatessen side dishes from her basket. 'I've brought lots of things in little pots,' she said. She would have to go shopping again before she went home.

They talked as they got the meal together, and went on talking as they sat at the kitchen table, eating, and drinking a cold white wine. It would have been pleasant, she thought, to have other meals like this, or just meet and chat sometimes. If Martin hadn't lived so far away they might have become friends. But he probably had enough friends already, not to mention girls who were stars in their own right.

'What's life with the Pomeroys like?' she asked.

'Don't knock them,' he said. 'They're the salt of the earth.'

'I know, I know. Nobody's got a social conscience bigger than Mrs Pomeroy's.' Lacey said that with affection. Mrs Pomeroy was a do-gooder who did good; and Martin began a wicked imitation of Edith reading out the morning paper to husband Edward whose responses were apparently limited to grunts. 'These mornings,' said Martin, 'she has me too.' He stabbed his fork towards Lacey. '"You were there, dear boy, why didn't you do something about it?" Often she means stop a war.'

He was part of the world that made headlines, and Lacey envied him the excitement, even the danger. She almost said, 'Write to me sometimes, tell me what's happening to you.' Then she remembered waiting for his letters and bit her lip and said, 'Porteus has got his voice back, but he says the paying customers would rather you were doing the acting,' and smiled. 'Whatever did your friends think about it?'

Martin laughed, 'Well . . .'

'I don't care,' she said. 'We're packing 'em in in Chadsford. I suppose Sandra Scott wouldn't take on Sweet Alice?'

'She had to get back to London.'

'Pity.' She wondered when, and could think of no questions that wouldn't sound prying, and began to tell him about the steak she had taken home on Monday night. Not that she had tried to ring him at the Cross Keys and invite him to come and share it, but that her father wasn't home, so she had collected Jet and she and the dog had feasted together.

She described Jet, hair on end, snarling like a werewolf, and her father yammering on about him having rabies, and Lacey trying to smooth down his hackles, and look him in the eye and tell him that her father was a friend.

'He didn't believe me,' she said.

'Not a friendly fellow, your father,' said Martin, and so far as Martin was concerned Laurence Allen was unfriendly. But he had a wide circle of admirers, he was well liked, and Lacey said defensively, 'Usually he is. He's just selective.' That was tactless, but she hadn't meant Martin, she thought her father was mistaken there. She meant other people who bored him or annoyed him or didn't agree with him. She said, 'He was a good friend to your father,' and when Martin agreed,

'So he was. We mustn't forget that, must we?' she sensed something she couldn't pin down and might have imagined. 'How about taking the coffee into the drawing room?' he said, and got up and began to put the cups on a tray. Lacey watched him for a moment, then she said, 'If you like.'

Mrs Pomeroy's drawing room was as elegant and luxurious as the rest of the house, but it was not one of Lacey's favourite rooms, because on the wall, behind the long couch in sea-green silk, hung the tapestry.

Other times when she had been in this room Lacey had usually managed to take a seat with her back to it. She hated the thing, which was one of Mrs Pomeroy's treasured keepsakes.

But today Lacey took a chair facing it, because it would be as well to keep remembering the evenings when Aunt Helena had sat stitching that purple and cerise bird against the dark green foliage while she sat praying that the phone would ring. The words rose in her throat now. 'Why didn't you write?'

But that would sound emotional, just when the situation was being cooled. Besides excuses that were five years old would be stale, and she knew that he hadn't written because he hadn't wanted to write.

He was pouring the coffee. 'No milk,' she said, and thought, you can look after yourself, cook, pour the coffee; you don't wait for anyone else to do it. And she remembered how the girls who fancied him used to say mournfully, 'You can't *do* things for Martin. He won't *let* you.' He had always had that inner aloofness, as though he never depended on anyone else. He didn't seem to have changed in that, she wondered how close Sandra was to him and if she had been the Pomeroys' guest for the weekend too. She wondered where Sandra had slept, and when he handed her her coffee cup she stirred it so briskly that it splashed into the saucer.

'What about that photograph in the *Mercury*?' she asked suddenly.

'How about it?' They both grinned and winced, and she protested,

'You weren't too bad, but I looked dreadful.'

'Well, it was a nasty moment, wasn't it?' His eyes gleamed wickedly. 'We could have been up there all night,' and again she felt near dangerous ground and rattled on,

'The reporter came down to the Centre. I don't know what kind of story she was after, but I think she decided there wasn't one. She told us your friends had arrived. How long did they stay?'

'They went back yesterday.' He was in the chair near to her, they were both deep easy chairs, but Lacey sat upright looking ahead while he lounged back, watching her.

So Sandra was here for Saturday and Sunday, and when they were together Lacey bet that Martin was never knocked breathless because some other girl looking a little like Lacey strolled by. She bet Martin never gave her a thought all weekend. That was probably why he was cool and friendly with her now, because Sandra's chemistry was a lot more potent. 'Have a nice weekend?' she enquired in social tones.

'Yes, thank you. Did you?' She could feel him watching her as she looked at the tapestry. 'Well,' she said, 'it's always a pleasant change by the sea.'

'You were at the sea?' He hadn't known that, and why should he unless he had asked after her, which he obviously had not?

'I went to Eastbourne. Paul's folk live there.'

'You went with Paul?'

'Of course.' This was the kind of conversation that must have been heard in this room hundreds of times to the chink of coffee cups. Polite chit-chat, verging on the boring because Martin was not really interested in her weekend. Although he asked, as one would, 'What did you do?' and she replied automatically, 'We went down to the beach, it was lovely weather. We saw a show. You know, just a seaside weekend.'

'Did you make love?'

Lacey almost dropped her cup, flushing angrily. She almost demanded 'Did you?' but she was not jealous, just affronted. It was time to get out, because he might be amusing himself, making her lose her temper. Or he could have been lulling her into a sense of false security and still intent on seduction. Either way she was having none of it.

She put down her half-empty coffee cup on the floor beside her chair and stood up and said 'Thanks for the meal, and what Paul and I do is none of your business. Just ours. Just between us. I told you I was marrying him.'

If Martin believed that he must let her go. He stood up too and said, 'Come here,' and she almost did. It would have needed no more than three steps, and she felt herself sway. Then she shook her head. And then she was afraid to move at all, for his hands were on her shoulders, his furious face close to her frightened one. 'Why won't you let me love you?' he said, and his hands were hurting her. 'What are you afraid of? Why are you such a coward? If you're planning spending the rest of your life hiding behind Paul the next few days should show if he's got what it takes to keep you safe from me.'

Paul hasn't, she thought. I'm the only one who can keep me safe from you, and I'm a coward because I know how it would be afterwards. Every stitch in that damned tapestry had stabbed at her heart.

'You don't want Paul,' he said. His voice was low but there was a terrifying violence in it, and he shook her, not hard, just jolting her, but she felt as though she had been hurled against the wall. Her head jerked back and from somewhere within her she found a voice. 'How do you know what I want, what I value? This is nothing— this skin-deep wanting.' He kissed her, engulfing her, crushing her to him, and from his kiss every part of her came awake; skin, blood, bone, every nerve and every fibre as though she was totally possessed. 'How deep did that go?' he asked, and his eyes seemed black and burning and she shut her eyes against them, and shook her head and fought for a moment with tight-shut eyes, beating fists against him.

When he released her she jumped back, kicking the coffee cup but not looking down. She began to babble, 'So I'm Sweet Alice, and I'm saying "Shove off" and

I'm meaning it, so how about trying to get the message?'

'Don't talk such bloody rubbish!' Martin shouted at her, and she ran out of the room, across the hall and out of the house, because she almost believed that he was angry enough to kill her.

She remembered her basket before she was out of the gate, but she couldn't go back for it. Nor for her wallet which was still in the basket. She would never have expected Martin to loose his self control like that in a million years. That's what came of being born a winner. You never thought you might come across anything you wanted that you couldn't get, especially when it had fallen like a ripe plum last time.

If he had followed she would have gone on running, although she was sure that the moment she was out of that room he would have himself in check again. Before he came out of the house the anger would be masked.

It had been like seeing a mask slip. She had never associated Martin with violence, although he lived with it for much of his working life. She had known he was an athlete as well as academically brilliant, an all-out all-rounder, but she had never seen him use his strength against anyone, and she was shaken at how close he had come to using it on her.

She couldn't go back to the Centre like this, somebody might spot that something was wrong with her. She couldn't face a second lunch in any of the pubs or snack bars, and if she went home her father could be there and start questioning her. But she had half an hour to kill before she was needed at the theatre, so she walked up on to the hills, where the air blew cooler on her burning cheeks.

She went in the opposite direction from the hut. She would never go there again, *never*, and she kept walking until it was time to retrace her steps. Her head was pounding and she wished fervently that she could have dodged this afternoon's matinee. It was too late now, but this was her final performance. She would lose her voice, or sprain her ankle, think up some excuse that no one could disprove, and there were plenty of girls who would be delighted to step into Alice's silver-buckled shoes. Lacey was doing no more play-acting opposite Martin. She had learned her lesson now, and she *would* keep out of his way.

The rows of seats were filling again, and Lacey wriggled out of her everyday clothes into the dimity gown with the puffed sleeves and petticoats. Everybody else in the dressing room seemed to be chattering around her like magpies. She wouldn't have been surprised to hear that Martin hadn't turned up. If he was that mad with her he could wash his hands of them all. But he must have come, because nobody said he hadn't, and the clock edged round towards two, and the ballad singer started his song and the curtain rose.

She tried to look at Martin as little as possible, playing her part, keeping her distance, although he was hardly likely to grab her in earnest in the middle of the stage. He was angry still. Behind the smooth face and the heavy-lidded eyes she could sense a contained rage.

What had she done to him, except prefer another man? And what right had he to consider himself insulted when he would have preferred Sandra to Lacey if Sandra had been here? This was male pride running rampant. She had always known he was an arrogant bastard. Maybe somehow this rejection would sink into his subconscious and teach him a little humility.

She couldn't wait to get the last scene over, with the flashing lights and the crashing of tinned thunder. She did her pleading and said her piece, and then she was standing close and facing him and he had to say, 'Why did you not reply to my messages? The time for mock modesty is over my proud beauty. You know the price.'

He spoke this loudly enough as a rule to reach the

back row easily, but now suddenly and unaccountably
his voice dropped so that it was doubtful if even the
front row could hear. And instead of, 'Why did you not
reply to my messages?' he asked. 'Why did you never
answer my letters?'

CHAPTER SEVEN

LACEY gasped, 'What?' and Martin said, 'You heard,' and that was where Freddy-as-William came charging in, swirling his axe, and Alice was supposed to faint.

She scrambled away while the two men mimed for the shadow show, and then all the players came hurrying on stage for their final bows, and Freddy was holding one of Lacey's hands and Martin the other. She had the fixed grin of a ventriloquist's dummy, but Martin wasn't pretending to smile. Nor was he looking at the audience, he was looking at Lacey. The applause was loud and long, and she muttered, 'You never wrote.'

'Twice,' he said. The rest of the cast were smiling out at the audience so that none of them even noticed the startled jerk of Lacey's head.

Where to? she wondered. But the address she had had then was home. This was years before the Centre came into being. She said, 'I got no letters from you,' and his expression was cynical.

'Then how come you asked me to stop writing when I phoned?'

'You *phoned*?' She had had no phone calls, she had told him nothing. The clapping went on, but she could hear him clearly although he spoke quietly.

'Miss Allen told me you had nothing to say to me.'

'Aunt Helena?' It was getting crazier. He had to be making it up. And this was where Alice and the squire and William stepped forward together, out of the ranks. Martin smiled then, and it was a smile she remembered where his eyes stayed watchful. 'The very one,' he said.

The curtain came down on its last descent for this performance, and everyone was milling around and her head was swimming so that she would have had difficulty in spelling her own name. What he had just said left a dozen questions unanswered, and heading the list—why should he lie, but now could he be telling the truth?

He still had her hand and Doreen, the producer, who had lived here all her life, said, grinning, 'It was true, wasn't it, that you two couldn't stand the sight of each other in the old days? Sworn enemies, weren't you?'

Everybody who knew them then remembered their antagonism, but Martin laughed now, raised the hand he held and kissed it. 'Shall we tell her what you and I were in the old days?' he said, and Lacey's face flamed under the greasepaint until it seemed that her whole body was one burning blush.

He was as good as announcing that he and she had been lovers, and her tongue was sticking to the roof of her mouth, and it seemed that everybody was staring and listening. She should laugh here and say something jokey—anything would do. If she hadn't turned scarlet they would have thought Martin was joking, but she was a picture of guilt, although there was nothing to feel guilty about. No one had been hurt but herself, and so long after it would have created only the mildest of sensations if it hadn't been so unexpected.

But everyone had been surprised at the rapid development of rapport between Martin Jackson and Lacey since he came back here. He had homed in on her that very first morning, and if they had had an affair, so secret that nobody suspected, before he left Chadsworth, well, that would explain a lot.

Lacey could read their thoughts, in the few seconds she stood with Martin's fingers gripping hers. If her mind had been clearer she might have said, 'What nonsense you talk,' admitting nothing. But instead she said, 'A lot of water has gone under the bridge since then.' She seemed to be saying that a lot and it was a stupid cliché, but the roaring in her head was like rushing water, and she was as dizzy as if she was spinning around in a whirlpool.

As she sat down in the dressing room her reflection in the mirror was framed by other faces. 'Was Martin Jackson an old flame of yours?' one of the faces was asking, and Lacey said,

'He had so many old flames in this town he's getting them mixed up,' although it was too late to take that tone now. Tessa, a pixie-faced girl, had been one of those who thought Martin was wonderful. She said ruefully, 'He was never serious about any of us.'

He was never serious about me, Lacey could have told her. He didn't write, he couldn't have done. She started to ease off her wig and knew that they were all adjusting to this new situation.

'And of course,' Tessa pounced, 'the festival was your idea in the first place, wasn't it?'

Now they were actually wondering if Lacey had planned it all just to get Martin back to Chadsford, and when she protested, 'Well, it wasn't my idea to invite him to open it,' she was promptly told,

'No, but he was a pretty obvious choice.' They thought she had been sly and deep, but she had their grudging admiration. 'I suppose it isn't serious?' said Tessa, and Lacey answered honestly,

'When he leaves here I don't suppose we shall see each other again for another five years,' and most of them nodded at that, agreeing with her.

'Well, I think you're dead lucky,' said another girl. 'Give you something to remember during the winter. I wouldn't mind having him, even if it was only for a fortnight—he's awfully sexy, isn't he?'

Hilarity took over, the talk became bawdy, and Lacey hurried. She was due for a hard time, from goodnatured teasing to invasion of privacy. That night with Martin had been locked inside her, so secret that she had almost hidden it from herself. She would never have discussed it with a living soul, but he had told them all, laughing.

That was proof enough that it hadn't meant much to him, but if he had written, and phoned, they might have gone on as friends. It was all speculation, but if she could be sure about the letters she would feel happier.

He said Aunt Helena had spoken to him, so perhaps her father would know, and as soon as she was in her own clothes, with most of her make-up removed, she made for the door. They asked her where she was dashing off to, and she said she was in a hurry. She ran most of the way home. Her father might not be there, but she would wait until he came, and if the phone rang she wouldn't answer it.

It could be any of a dozen friends who couldn't believe what they had just heard, that Lacey and Martin had had something going in the old days. And again now, of course. Sandra Scott had been here over the weekend and Lacey had gone away with Paul, but now everybody would be convinced that off-stage activities were accounting for the sizzling sex scenes in *Sweet Alice*.

Most of the women would envy her, although some might be malicious. Her father would be shocked, and Paul would be hurt. She had wanted to free herself from Paul as gently as possible, not under this fierce spotlight, and the eyes of everyone in town who knew them. There must be some way of saving Paul's pride. She must think about it, that much she owed him, but right now the only thing on her mind was the letters.

The back door of the house was unlocked and she went from room to room on the ground floor, searching for her father. His studio was empty too, and she stood looking around her. It was all familiar: the smell of paints, the big north windows, the easel, the canvasses propped against the walls. The desk, the sofa, the chairs, the fireplace where a fire burned from the first autumnal chill. Laurence Allen disliked piped heating, and Lacey had been carrying logs and coal up here since she was ten years of age.

She had wanted to go away, and Aunt Helena had known that. There had been that scene on the night of the storm. Martin was the one who got away, breaking his father's heart, Lacey's father had said, but this little town had been too small to hold him, and perhaps the first letter had been opened in error. If Martin had written affectionately, perhaps mentioning the wider world outside Lacey's cloistered existence, that could have read like heresy to Aunt Helena. Who would carry the coals up to the studio with Lacey gone?

Then a second letter, and a phone call. He could have said he would ring, and Aunt Helena could have got up from her tapestry and taken the call and come back and picked up her needle, and gone on stabbing and stitching.

That was how it could have happened, and how Lacey wanted it to have been. She would like to think that Martin had meant to keep in touch, and she had always known that Aunt Helena considered Laurence Allen's work more important than the happiness of anyone else in this house. But Aunt Helena would probably have discussed this with him. Not much was allowed to trouble him, but Lacey felt she would have mentioned it before she answered Martin's phone call with a downright lie.

None of her father's best work was here today, that was at his exhibition in the local art gallery, and he strolled down there most afternoons, enjoying the flattery of being recognised.

Lacey went into the bathroom and cleared the residue of greasepaint from her face and combed her hair, and she was sitting in the drawing room, door to the hall ajar, when she heard the front door opening. This was going to be grim, but she had to do it. She came across the carpet out into the hall, almost bumping into her father and startling him. 'I wasn't expecting you home so early,' he said.

'I came straight from the theatre.'

'I haven't managed to see the play yet.' He was wearing a grey suit with a tie in a lighter grey that matched the silvery thatch of his hair. His coat was cashmere, he always dressed like a dandified actor. 'But I've heard about it. Martin Jackson seems to be giving the rôle his own interpretation.'

He was passing her by, going towards the staircase, when she said, 'I'm worried about something Martin's just told me,' and that halted him. 'He said he wrote to me a couple of times after he left Chadsford, but I never got any letters.'

Her father's eyebrows rose. 'Well?'

'Do you remember anything about them?'

'Letters?' He had looked blank until then, but suddenly his face darkened. 'From Martin Jackson to you? Why should he be writing to you?'

'He also said he phoned and spoke to Aunt Helena, and she asked him to stop writing.'

'Helena did?' Now he was bewildered again.

'I thought it sounded unlikely at first, but——'

'Why was he writing to you?' Her father returned to the point he considered of overriding importance. 'You and he were never friendly.' All this seemed to be news to him, so perhaps her aunt had kept it to herself. He waited for Lacey's reply and getting none persisted sharply, 'Were you?'

'Yes,' she said, turning to walk back into the drawing room, deep in thought.

'How friendly?'

'Very.' Laurence Allen gulped and gasped, then followed her, demanding,

'What do you mean, very? You always gave me the impression you disliked him as much as I did. I know there's been some talk about the pair of you since he came back here, but are you telling me now that there was anything going on before, that you and he were——' He paused as though the word would choke him, and Lacey snapped,

'That's right.' If she didn't tell him somebody else might, Paul for one, and his face was mottling as he spat out,

'You and Martin Jackson? I can't believe it! That's appalling, unspeakable! His father used to worry about the girls Martin treated like dirt, but I never for one moment imagined that my own daughter could be one of his cast-offs. You let him——' He shuddered, and spluttered, 'have you no pride, no shame?'

She could have shouted him down, she was angry enough. But she forced herself to keep quiet because the shock had been traumatic for him. He had this deep-seated loathing of Martin, and now Lacey was admitting an affair. If one night qualified. But saying, 'Only one night,' might only make it sound wilder, and as her father went ranting on about her unspeakable behaviour she couldn't even say, 'It could never happen again.'

'He says he wrote to you does he? And you say you never got the letters?' She nodded to both questions. 'And how long ago was this?'

'When the Jackson house was sold.'

'And the phone call your aunt was supposed to have answered?'

'The same time.'

'He wrote no letters to you.' Laurence Allen's voice rang with scorn. 'Your aunt would never open anyone else's correspondence, nor lie about anything. You know that as well as I do.' Lacey would have thought not, but what other explanation was there?

'After he left here,' her father said contemptuously, 'he never bothered to keep in touch with you. And he won't when he leaves again. You're infatuated. I suppose that was the reason before, but you were how old then? Eighteen? Nineteen? At that age I suppose there was some excuse, but my God, girl, I should have thought you'd have learned some common sense by now!'

He went out of the room, slamming the door, and Lacey sighed, because that was the simplest explanation of all, that Martin was lying. As Aunt Helena was dead nothing could be proved either way, and Lacey would have to make up her own mind. 'I should have thought you'd have learned some common sense by now,' her father had just said, but common sense hardly entered into it. She had to go on instinct, gut reaction, maybe wishful thinking because she wanted Martin to have written those letters.

The roses that he had sent her a week ago were still blooming and perfect. Her father didn't know where they had come from or he would have thrown them out, but she went to the bowl now and breathed in their fragrance. They hadn't much longer to go before their petals fell, but for a few more days they would be so beautiful that perhaps she would remember them for the rest of her life.

She called at the wool shop to collect Jet on her way to the Centre. Mrs Bowden was sitting down with a cup of tea in the living room, an ear cocked for the ringing of the bell over the shop door, when Lacey walked in.

'Cup of tea?' she offered, as she peered into the shop and saw Lacey.

'Thanks, but I have to get back.' Lacey had had Mrs Bowden's tea before. It was liquorice-black and she didn't feel she could stomach it this afternoon. 'Missed me?' she asked the dog, who was carrying on as though she had been away for weeks.

'Don't you worry about him,' said Mrs Bowden. 'He's been doing all right—Martin Jackson took him for a walk yesterday.'

'On his own, was he, Martin?' Lacey enquired casually, and Mrs Bowden hesitated, then said,

'I think there was somebody with him. A young lady, I think. She's on television too, isn't she?'

Sandra Scott, who would be sharing Martin's life again next week, but who had left town last night.

Lacey scratched Jet under the chin, and thought, I wish you could talk, then you could tell me where you went, what they said to each other. And then, No, I don't—I don't want to know.

'I went to Eastborne for the weekend,' she said brightly.

'I like Blackpool myself,' said Mrs Bowden.

'Good job you do,' said Lacey, 'Or we wouldn't have had Jet.'

I like it here, she thought, coming out of the shop with the dog loping along beside her. This town, this week. I won't think about next week, because maybe he did write to me five years ago, and when he goes away again there'll be nothing to stop me writing to him.

She reached the square and looked across at the library, wondering how the news would reach Paul that Martin had announced this afternoon that they had all been fooled if they thought that he and Lacey hadn't been very good friends in the old days.

The old days were no big deal today, but this contrasted so completely with everything Lacey had said that Paul would probably be as appalled as her father was. Her father had called it unspeakable that she and Martin should ever have been close, and she would find that hard to forgive. He had accused her of having no pride, but he was wrong. She had pride and spirit, and from now on she was hiding behind nobody.

She went into the Centre by the side door, and in the first workroom two girls were painting tiny blue flowers on china saucers. 'Hey,' the one nearest the door called to her, 'was he joking?'

'Who?' asked Lacey.

'Were you?' They were both smiling, and she laughed.

'Don't you mean, are we?'

That was the question—whether she and Martin were lovers now—and a mood of devilment was on her.

Upstairs Maisie got her at the first chance of a quiet word, to ask, 'Is it a fact?'

'Five years after,' said Lacey, 'what does it matter?'

'Nothing,' said Maisie. 'If he hadn't come back.'

But Martin had come back, and there had never been anyone to whom Lacey had felt so irresistibly drawn. She had known that as soon as he walked across to her that first morning, and if she believed in the letters—and she had made up her mind, she was believing—then she was going to live a little during what was left of the festival.

She was sure she would be seeing him this evening. She knew he would get in touch, and she was called to the phone twice before the Centre closed to the public. But not by Martin. One was a business call, the other was Denice, who was aghast and outraged, and Lacey was shaken to learn how quickly the gossip had spread, or what it had gained in the telling. Denice had heard that Lacey and Martin had not only had a passionate and secret love affair before he left Chadsford, but had spent several holidays together since in some very exotic places.

'Tahiti?' Lacey shrilled. 'You're sure they don't mean Torbay? I've never been within a thousand miles of Tahiti!'

'Did you go to Torbay with Martin?' squealed Denice.

'Of course I didn't. I hadn't seen him for five years.'

'I thought it was funny the way you were smiling at him at our party.'

'I wasn't. Oh, what does it matter?' Lacey sighed. 'I have to go.'

Martin came up the stairs when the magistrates' court was closing. Most of the stallholders had shut up shop, and the last of the customers were leaving, and Lacey had been busying herself in her corner, but she saw him reach the top of the stairs and she sat down on her stool. No hurrying, she had resolved, no running to meet him. Keep them guessing. And him.

Martin couldn't be sure of his reception. There had been that row over lunch, and not much conversation between them since, although the little that had been said was momentous. Lacey kept a perfectly straight face, crossed her ankles and tucked them under the stool, hands folded demurely in her lap. Jet got up from his bed on the rug behind the stall, tail swishing a welcome as Martin reached them. 'Coming?' asked Martin.

She wouldn't like him to know how hard it was for her to sit still and not reach out to touch him, but she couldn't help smiling and so did he. 'Hang about,' she said.

'Sure.'

There were things she had to do before she left, and now he was here she could get on with them. It was her turn to sweep the place out. They were all responsible for their own stalls and workrooms, but they ran a rota who picked up and swept up each evening, and now Lacey went to fetch a big black plastic bag and a broom from the cupboard in the storeroom, while Martin wandered around.

Upstairs usually emptied before downstairs. The workrooms were used until all hours, but soon Martin and Lacey were the only two up here. Porteus and Maisie were the last to go, calling 'Goodnights' and grinning broadly; and as they clattered down the iron staircase Lacey said, 'You've started the tongues wagging. It's going around now that we've been off on secret jaunts together for years.'

Martin was sitting on the top of three shallow steps that led to a raised platform at the end of the room. This was where the magistrates had once overlooked the court. Now it was the jewellery department of four stalls. He sat with long legs jack-knifed, watching her pick up the squashed plastic cups, lolly sticks and crisp packets, and drop them into her black sack. 'Why were we keeping them secret?' he asked.

'I don't know. But Denice phoned and said somebody had told her I went to Tahiti with you.' She gave a muted shriek. '*Tahiti*, of all places! Have you been to Tahiti?'

'Yes, as a matter of fact. I went last year with some friends who had a boat.'

Someone local who knew that must have decided now that Lacey was a likely crew member. Chance would have been a fine thing, she thought wistfully, and wondered who the friends were. And if it was Sandra in those days, or an earlier girl-friend who swam with Martin in blue sparkling waters, or lay on white sands under waving palm trees.

'Well, I haven't,' she said. 'Does it look like the photographs?'

'Yes. Where *have* you been?'

'In the last five years?' She turned, leaning on her broom, pulling a face. 'Are you serious? I haven't been anywhere. On holidays, yes, away for a couple of weeks. But this is the first time anyone's suggested I'm leading a racy life.'

Martin laughed. 'You look as if you have. There's something rakehelly about you, Miss Allen, even when you're holding a broom. It must be something to do with your hair.'

The unruly halo, like his. She remembered him saying that wasn't all they had in common, that they were two of a kind, and for the few days she had left she might even try living up to that. She said, 'I still find it hard to believe you wrote to me, let alone phoned.'

'Checkmate,' he said. 'I'm not entirely sold on the idea that you didn't get them.' Lacey could hear voices downstairs, but nothing anyone else was saying mattered. 'Suppose,' Martin suggested, 'we both believe what we want to believe.'

'Right.' That was what she would do, take what she was offered, with no guarantees. He would never be committed in the way she was, but she would have something to remember through the winter, like the girl said, and maybe Martin would come back again for next year's festival. Something between pain and rueful laughter gripped her, and she started sweeping vigorously, raising an unnecessary amount of dust.

'Is this one of your regular jobs?' Martin enquired.

'Tonight's my turn.' She went straight on, 'What had you in mind for later?'

'I thought we might get out of town. Drive off somewhere.' And not come back till morning. That didn't need saying, she understood what he meant. Luckily she had her weekend case.

'Let's do that,' she said lightly as though it would be pleasant but nothing earth-shattering.

She didn't look at him because she didn't want to see even the slightest sign of triumph, as though he had won the game. If she didn't look she could pretend it wasn't a game, and after a moment he asked, 'Can I help?'

She was sweeping a pile of dust and small debris into a long-handled dustpan. 'You could give the iron work a rub-up,' she said.

'Where do you keep your dusters?' A low wrought-iron balustrade, painted black, edged the platform. Lacey brought him dusters and he dusted and polished while she got on with her clearing up. She laughed across, from the far end of the room, as he stood back surveying his efforts. 'Not bad at all. Do you do your own housework?'

She was joking, but he said, 'That depends. I live in a service flat in London, but I've got a cottage on Carra. When I'm there I shift for myself.'

Who do you take along with you? she wondered, and pictures came into her head of a wild coastline and Martin and a girl walking over the rocks, beside the sea. And inside a cottage with a peat fire and a lamp burning, rough-hewn furniture, and through an open door a shadowy room and a wide bed.

'Tell me about your cottage,' she said, and he described it, and she could see it as he talked, but she couldn't ask, 'Who goes with you?'

Time must have passed. They were in no hurry. Lacey went leisurely about her chores because she liked being here, she was fond of her little property. She often came back, in the evening, just to check that all was well, or to talk for a while with anybody who was still working.

Tonight, with Martin here, the great high-vaulted room seemed a particularly pleasing place. He did some shopping, starting with a woven rug that had that afternoon gone up on the wall behind one of the stalls. 'I like that,' he said, so Lacey took him into the storeroom to see half a dozen others and make his selection, which turned out to be the first one, although they discussed each pattern at length. Then he decided to buy one of Porteus's bread vats, and some green glass goblets, and when the phone began to ring faintly in the office below Lacey said, 'Someone will get it.' Her friends would be pleased at the sales, and the more Martin took back with him from here the harder it would be for him to forget Lacey's market.

But no one downstairs was rushing to answer, because the phone went on ringing, and Lacey said reluctantly, 'I suppose I'd better go, but I hope it isn't for me.' Most of all she hoped it wasn't Paul. There was absolutely nothing she could say to Paul right now. She was halfway down the stairs when the ringing stopped, and she waited to hear if her name was called.

It wasn't. There wasn't a sound, and although it was not yet dark dusk was falling fast. They had switched on the lights upstairs, but there were no lights down here, just an all-pervading feeling of emptiness. Lacey began to open doors on to empty rooms. The doors leading outside were locked, and she slowly went upstairs again, where Martin was examining a toad carved in soapstone, and told him, 'A slight problem. We're locked in.'

'How?'

'It should be foolproof. Everybody who had a stall has a key to the side door. After six o'clock they lock as they leave. Porteus and Maisie have keys to the office and the front door as well. They've gone—well, everybody's gone, and now we're locked in.'

Martin raised an eyebrow. 'Foolproof?'

'Of course, I have a set of keys. Only I left them in my wallet in the Pomeroys' kitchen. You didn't——?'

He shook his head. 'Sorry. What about the phone?'

'That's in the office. So is the safe, you see, and the money gets left in that overnight, so we——'

'Lock the office.'

'Uh-huh. You can get out into the exercise yard.'

'Where the walls are about fourteen feet high.'

'Thereabouts.' And a sheer drop the other side.

'Well,' said Martin, 'we can always walk the dog.'

She couldn't decide whether this was funny or infuriating. 'Somebody will probably come back,' she said. 'They do. They come in and out as they like. Some of them work till after midnight, sometimes.'

Martin checked his watch and it was later than she'd thought, and tonight could be the night that nobody returned. She had left the lights on in the corridor, but it was awfully quiet down there. You could hear the noise of the fair if you listened, and Jet was snuffling up here as if he was on the track of something along the wainscoting.

'How's the window situation?' asked Martin.

'The office is the only window that opens on to the road. Most of the others down there have bars on them.' It was a long time since this had been a jail. Not in living memory. But the little rooms that had been storerooms, and workrooms since Lacey opened her Centre, were designed as cells, and for the first time she felt the pressure of claustrophobia closing in on her.

Several high narrow pointed windows up here had ventilation vents at the top. You pulled a cord to open them, and Martin suggested, 'We might try lobbing an S.O.S. through.'

'You're not smashing my leaded lights,' said Lacey. 'Things aren't that desperate.'

'Who's desperate?' he drawled, and laughed. 'So we're locked in. So relax and enjoy it.'

'Well,' she said, 'I love it here. I mean, this is my very favourite building. But I've never spent a whole night here before. The mod-cons don't include sleeping quarters.'

'You expect to be sleeping?' No, she did not, but it was fun to fool.

'It's a hard floor,' she said. 'Would you like to borrow Jet's blanket?'

'We'll shop around before we deprive him.' His arm round her shoulders was comfortable and casual and completely right. Anything would be good if we were touching, Lacey thought, from walking down the street to making love. Just the feel of him brought such comfort and delight. 'This isn't quite what I had in mind,' he said, 'but as jails go it seems very well equipped.'

'Someone will come.' There was a fifty-fifty chance. It would be nice if somebody did, because she would have preferred a more romantic and luxurious setting. She would rather drive out of town and find a quiet room where nothing would disturb them till morning.

'While we're waiting——' said Martin. He turned her towards him, looking deep into her eyes, and she put her arms around his neck and offered her parted lips to him. This time he kissed her gently, and she melted in a lovely surge of sensuous warmth until a sudden clattering like machinegun fire shattered the silence.

Jet was banging his tin dish around in the corner. Usually Lacey had fed him long before now. He was getting hungry and he stopped the kissing. Which was as well, because almost certainly the kiss would have led to better things, and Lacey would not have cared for any of her colleagues to have arrived on that scene. Gossip was one thing, eye-witnesses were another.

'While we're waiting,' she said breathlessly, 'I think we ought to forage for some food.'

'What do you give him?'

Jet came out from behind her stall with his dish. He might not fare too well if they were stuck here overnight, because she only had some dog biscuits for him. She took the carton from a drawer and shook a few into the dish. 'If we get out,' she said, 'do we take him home?'

'We'll take him with us,' said Martin. 'He's on our side, he won't grass.' He watched the munching dog and declared, 'I could eat a horse!'

'Hush!' Lacey put her hands over Jet's ears, and was surprised to realise how hungry she was herself. Somebody had to have left something edible. They often ate as they worked in here, bringing in food. Surely there would be the odd packet of biscuits around.

She started to hunt, on shelves under the stalls, in cupboards and drawers. This was an emergency, she would apologise in the morning, but she wasn't making much of a haul. There were some biscuits, three separate half-empty packs; a tube of fruit gums, a broken bar of chocolate, some extra strong mints and a packet of sunflower seeds.

'Sweet-toothed tastes,' Martin remarked, as they surveyed their booty, and Lacey told him, 'We might do better downstairs. Porteus is a secret eater. He hides it in the pottery room, and tries to fool Maisie. Then he comes up with crumbs in his beard.'

In the pottery room they found half a small pork pie, that looked fresh and smelt safe. Lacey produced it with a flourish of triumph. 'About three mouthfuls apiece. If we eat slowly here's our main course.'

Jet was right with her. He had been keeping very close as they rooted around in the little rooms, and now he shoved a shaggy head between her and the piece of pie she held at arm's length, and Martin said, 'I think his need's greater.'

'This is your lot,' Lacey warned the dog, who saw the pie off in three seconds flat and continued to follow them around, as close as a shadow, while they collected a packet of bacon-flavoured crisps, some chewing gum, a jar of chutney and a bottle of Coke. Coffee and tea and an electric kettle were fixtures in the kitchenette, but there was an unopened bottle of home-made damson wine in the wood carving room.

'They won't begrudge us a drop of this,' said Lacey. It was going to be the joke of the year tomorrow—Lacey Allen getting locked in the old jail overnight with Martin Jackson. Her father wouldn't be amused, but she hadn't intended going home tonight anyway, and her father's approval had ceased to matter to her. Paul was another who wouldn't laugh. Neither would Denice. And there was still time, of course, for someone to let them out, but that hope was receding, and unless somebody came with a key there was no escape.

The doors of black fumed oak were so thick that you could batter away on the inside without any sound getting through. Front and side locks had been changed to Yales when the building became a warehouse, but the door to the exercise yard relied on the old bolts and wooden bars, fastening from the inside.

While Lacey was examining the handwritten label on the bottle of wine Martin opened the door to the yard and Jet padded out, a pale restless shape prowling between the shrouded stalls.

It was a little yard, backing on to the hillside that sloped away. A place of shadows within the high walls. The sky was edged with a pinkish glow from the lights of the town and the lights of the fair, but when Lacey stepped outside and looked up stars sparkled against blackness so brightly that they dazzled her.

Martin stood framed in the narrow doorway. Lacey had moved away and she couldn't see him clearly, not his face, his expression, only the outline of broad shoulders and dark curly hair. She wanted to say, 'I love you,' but that wouldn't be clever. 'It's quite a night for stars,' she said. 'If it was less murky out here we could dine under them. What do you think Jet's after?'

'Rats?' suggested Martin.

Likely enough. Old buildings had them. Round here they would be country rats from the fields, not your sewer variety; all the same, 'Sorry I mentioned it,' she said, and called the dog, who came from under one of the stalls and trotted back into the building, waiting for them just inside the door.

'So where do we settle?' Lacey mused. 'It's more compact down here but more cluttered, and I don't think I fancy a night in a cell. And it's all stone, which is colder. Upstairs, do you think? My corner could be quite comfortable. Tell you what,' she decided, 'we'll put down your rug and we'll get some cushions.' Cushions came in all shapes and sizes. There was a pile of them in the storeroom.

She was suddenly activated, like somebody laying on an impromptu party. This was a silly thing to happen and a nuisance, but it could be fun, they could get a laugh out of it; and she would guard against the longing that had come over her, looking up at the stars, to say that she loved him.

She went to the stores and helped herself to beanbags and cushions and made a comfortable floor-level couch. Then she brought plates and arranged the eatables, while Martin opened the damson wine and poured a little into two of the green glass goblets.

'It's four years old, going by the label,' said Lacey. 'Does four years count for vintage with home-made?' She sipped and savoured. Martin's expression was wry, but she pronounced it, 'Quite nice. A bit thick and sweet. A bit like Ribena.'

'I think I'll stick with Coke,' said Martin.

They left most of the lights on until it was obvious that no one was coming back. Lacey had her overnight bag, so she could clean her teeth and take off her make-up. She could change into a nightdress if she chose, which she did not. But she would put on her towelling robe, because the room was big and barny and they hadn't bothered to renew the paraffin supply during the heatwave, and it might turn chilly in the night.

She reached for her small case and pulled out her yellow robe. 'Nobody's coming till morning,' she said.

'Looks that way,' Martin agreed.

'We might as well switch off the lights.'

The fairground music had stopped. They had eaten the crisps and most of the biscuits and talked away an hour or so. Lacey wanted to hear about his cottage. For some reason it fascinated her. He had had it for three years, he told her, finding it by sheer luck when he was in the Scottish islands covering a story. They were like old friends talking, who had lost touch for years, and together again found a sexual attraction between them that was strong and undeniable.

That was how Lacey felt. Beyond denial. Because there was no denying that from the top of her head to the tips of her toes every inch of her wanted Martin, and tonight they were touching again and it was time to turn out some of the lights. She took her toilet bag out of the case and said, 'I'll see to downstairs.'

She had hardly moved for over an hour. She had sat comfortably propped up among the beanbags and cushions, nibbling, drinking the damson wine, joking and talking. She felt relaxed and beautifully content. But when she stood her bones turned to water and her knees buckled, and Martin jumped up. 'Good grief!' she said faintly.

'Are you all right?'

'Of course I'm all right.' She picked her way carefully over the cushions on to the dark-stained floorboards. At the top of the staircase she transferred her toilet bag to her left hand. Her robe was draped over that, which left her right hand free to grip the balustrade as she walked down the iron stairs.

She *was* all right. She knew exactly what she was doing. She was heading first for the loo, then to clean her teeth. And while she was at the sink she would put her face in a bowl of cold water. And maybe before she did any of this she would fill the kettle and switch it on and make some extra strong coffee.

She had heard tales of home-made wine, but this hadn't tasted particularly potent. It had tasted smooth, and she had become progressively happier. She was still happy. She dropped robe and bag on the little table in the kitchenette and went along the corridor to the toilet, holding on to the wall. Then she cleaned her teeth and washed her face, with dogged determination, and looked at her bleary reflection in a little mirror that hung over the sink.

She was happy because Martin was here, waiting for her, but she felt sick. She couldn't make coffee, she daren't risk lifting a kettle of boiling water. She held on to the sink and she didn't hear him coming until he was standing behind her. Then she said jerkily, 'I think it was the wrong label. It should have read delayed action dynamite.'

'Coffee?' he asked.

'I just want to lie down.'

'O.K. Come on.' She went back upstairs with everything whirling around her. She knew he was helping her up, step after step, but everything was hazy until she collapsed into her nest of cushions in the corner again, and closed her eyes and tried to fight her way out of the mist, because tonight of all nights she had to stay awake.

Lights went out. She heard them clicking and the

brightness against her eyelids faded, and she tried
desperately to open her eyes. When she managed it she
saw the light filtering through the high windows and the
grotesque shadowy shapes of the stalls. It looked weird.
Martin sat beside her. She could have touched him if
she could have lifted her hand, and Jet howled like a
werewolf and the noise went right through her head,
making her groan, 'Oh no—oh, please shut him up!'

She saw Martin get up and turn on one of the lights
at the other end of the room so that the shapes were
stalls again. That reassured the dog, who stopped
howling, but Lacey couldn't fight the waves of sleep
that were crashing over her. She watched Martin
coming back. He seemed to move in slow motion, and
she couldn't keep her eyes open any longer. As they
closed she said, as loudly as she could because she
wanted him to hear, 'I'm so sorry. I do love you . . .'

Her head was splitting. 'Drink this,' said Martin.

'I don't want——' But it was daylight, morning, and
she asked, 'What time is it?' through stiff lips.

'Getting on for eight.'

Any time now they could start arriving and all Lacey
wanted to do was crawl into a dark cupboard. She took
the coffee in shaking hands and the cup clattered
against her teeth. 'I think I'm dying,' she moaned. 'How
much of that stuff did I drink?'

'Not all that much,' said Martin. 'It packs a kick.'

'I feel rough.'

'You look it.' He was grinning at her and she said,

'You need a shave.' He had cleared away plates,
debris, and most of the cushions. He had another mug
of coffee and he sat on her stool drinking it. Jet sat
beside him, bright-eyed, and she surveyed the pair
blearily. Then she said, 'There's a first-aid box in the
kitchen. Aspirins. Would you——?'

The first arrival was half an hour later, by which time
Lacey was moving around, but her head still ached and
she certainly couldn't stand the ribald comments that

would fill the morning here. Not until this afternoon at the earliest. 'As soon as anyone comes I'm going,' she said. 'I can't see the joke right now. Porteus chortling away would be the last straw.'

'Sure,' said Martin.

Anton, the woodcarver, was the first to open the side door and walk into the Centre. Lacey was in the kitchen, with her third mug of black coffee, and he said cheerily, 'Good morning.'

'That's a matter of opinion,' said Lacey. 'Was it your damson wine, the bottle in the workroom?'

He looked surprised, 'Yes. My cousin Lucy makes it.'

Martin and Jet came into the corridor from the exercise yard. 'I'll explain later,' Lacey said to Anton, and walked out of the Centre along the narrow passageway into the road.

'Where now?' asked Martin.

'I'm going home for an hour or two. I'm beginning to feel better, but I can't face that lot just yet. I'd like my keys, though.' She didn't want to face her father either. She wanted to get into her bedroom and be quiet and still for a while. Martin's car was parked just up the road. He opened the door and Lacey got into the passenger seat, while Martin hauled Jet into the back.

She had made such a fool of herself last night. It had all gone wrong when it could have been right. It wasn't funny at all, although she had to keep smiling. She said, 'Anton's cousin makes the damson wine. Her name's Lucy—short for Lucretia, I should think. What's Mrs Pomeroy going to say when I turn up at this hour and you're needing a shave?'

'You can stay in the car if you like,' he said. 'I'll get your wallet.'

But Mr Pomeroy was leaving for the office as Martin's car turned into the drive, Mrs Pomeroy was at the front door waving him off, and she came hurrying out when she saw them. 'You've just missed a phone call,' she told Martin. 'They rang last night and again just now. The number's on the pad. Oh, hello,' she beamed at Lacey. 'Come in and have a cup of coffee.'

Lacey followed into the kitchen. Her basket and wallet were on the welsh dresser, and she explained, 'I left them behind yesterday.'

'I thought they had to be yours,' said Mrs Pomeroy. The breakfast plates were still on the table, with a place laid for Martin. They knew he hadn't slept in this house, and while Mrs Pomeroy poured perked coffee Lacey said, 'My keys are in there. We got locked in the Centre all night.'

'Oh dear,' said Mrs Pomeroy. 'All night? Here, drink your coffee.'

Lacey was beginning to feel awash with coffee, but she gulped it down while Mrs Pomeroy gathered the plates and put them in the sink and refilled the water bowl for Sukey the fat old spaniel. She has something on her mind, thought Lacey. Something she wants to say. Mrs Pomeroy had quite an expressive face. It puckered every time she looked across at Lacey; and then Martin came into the kitchen and said, 'I have to leave right away.'

Lacey swallowed and a jagged lump that hurt terribly rose in her throat. 'I'll try to come back on Saturday,' he said. For the end of the festival, the day of the runaway mop. But he was going now and she had wasted last night. She said carefully,

'That would be nice if you could manage it.'

'I'll run you home.'

'Don't bother.' In her state she might burst into tears, which would be the blessed end.

'*I'll* take you,' Mrs Pomeroy declared. 'It won't be out of my way at all—I want to go to Goose Lane.' She grabbed a check jacket that hung behind the kitchen door and put it on, picked up Lacey's basket and said, 'Come along, then, dear child.'

Martin smiled, 'Goodbye.'

'Well, goodbye,' said Lacey.

'It's been fun seeing you again—and lay off the damson wine!'

She couldn't believe it. If she had felt less fragile she thought she would have said something else. Like 'Please come back'. She might have added, 'Must you go?' but she supposed he must or he wouldn't. He didn't try to stop her as she went off with Mrs Pomeroy and got into Mrs Pomeroy's little car, with Mrs Pomeroy rabbiting on about it being another lovely morning and how fortunate they'd been getting this kind of weather, sounding as smug as though she had organised the sunshine personally.

'I've left the dog in Martin's car,' said Lacey suddenly. 'Do you think I'd better go back for him?'

'No,' said Mrs Pomeroy. 'He'll get him to Mrs Bowden's.' She negotiated the main road and turned off towards Lacey's home. Then she said brusquely, 'Don't go back.'

'Why not?' and Lacey felt the tears sliding down her face. Mrs Pomeroy's gaze was fixed on the road, but she seemed to know how Lacey was feeling, and Lacey dabbed her cheeks with fingertips and then asked, 'Why ever not?' because it would only be Jet she was going back for, not Martin.

'A young lady phoned last night,' said Mrs Pomeroy, 'and this morning. Name of Sandra.' The car drew up outside the gates of Lacey's home and Lacey wanted to jump out and run, but she felt a hundred years old.

'It's all right,' she said, 'I know about Sandra.' And nobody was going to know how much it hurt that Martin was leaving because Sandra had phoned.

'Your aunt was one of my dearest friends,' said Mrs Pomeroy gruffly. 'That's why I'm telling you this. It isn't ethical and strictly speaking it isn't my business.' She was rarely at a loss for words, but she was now. Her expression was a mixture of apology and pity, as though she was the bearer of bad news she couldn't get out. Then she announced, 'I shouldn't like you getting too fond of Martin, because he's not going to let himself get involved with anyone of the name of Allen.'

Lacey sat staring at her, and Mrs Pomeroy sighed looking past Lacey to the dark windows of the house. 'It was a few years ago, of course, but it was a sizeable amount of money, and you are Laurence Allen's daughter, and it wasn't straight dealing.'

When she paused Lacey said, 'I haven't a clue what you're talking about,' and Mrs Pomeroy let go the driving wheel she had been clutching, raised her hands and let them fall, then said briskly and bluntly,

'Off the record, I'm talking about your father swindling his.'

CHAPTER EIGHT

'I DON'T believe you,' Lacey said, and heard herself almost laughing, although it was a lousy joke and Mrs Pomeroy was looking as grim as a judge. 'When?' asked Lacey. 'I mean, how?' She took a deep breath. 'He never did?'

'Oh yes, he did,' Mrs Pomeroy retorted. 'Take it from me. There's not many know, but Martin does, of course. And if you're going to ask your father outright watch his eyes, because he'll probably deny it, he's a crafty old fox.'

The sickness was back again. Lacey could have heaved as she bit her lip and said stonily, 'This is slander, you know.'

'Perhaps your father would care to sue me,' snapped Mrs Pomeroy, and softened at once, laying a gentle hand on Lacey's arm. 'It was a long time ago. Only you're a sensible girl and you must see that Martin Jackson isn't likely to forget it. You two have been seeing a lot of each other since he came back, haven't you, and I expect things have moved pretty fast—well, they do these days, don't they? I'm not a prude, I know the world's changed since I was a girl when we thought kissing was going it. But perhaps you shouldn't set too much store on seeing him again too soon. He said he might come back on Saturday, but I don't know——'

She meant that Lacey might be falling in love but Martin was not. He had cleared off now, back to Sandra, and if Lacey's father had defrauded his 'old friend' in the 'old days' Martin Jackson was not likely to be planning more than a brief encounter with Laurence Allen's daughter. Anyhow, Lacey had always known he would go. It had just happened a few days earlier than she had expected.

She said, 'Thank you for telling me. Although we both knew this wasn't serious. It was just—fun, you know.'

'Times have changed,' said Mrs Pomeroy sadly. 'I suppose I ought to be glad that nobody's getting hurt.'

Lacey watched the car move away before she turned to walk through the gates. Her head was throbbing agonisingly and she thought—Nothing really changes. Nothing real.

She opened the front door and her father came into the hall. He was shaved and talced, and spruced up for the day, and had probably discovered in the last ten minutes that she was not in the house and that her bed might not have been slept in. 'Where have you been?' he demanded.

'I got locked in the Centre,' she told him. 'I didn't have my keys with me.' He took a moment to assimilate that and what it might mean, and she went on quietly, 'Was it your fault that Courtney Jackson died poor?'

'Watch his eyes,' Mrs Pomeroy had said, but Lacey wasn't seeing too clearly herself. Pain was blurring her vision. She saw him stiffen and scowl and flush angrily. Or guiltily. Then he blustered, 'Did Jackson say that?' Lacey faced him tight-lipped and he mumbled, 'There was a small business deal that fell through. Through no fault of mine. It was Martin who got the money.'

Lacey was sure it was not. She couldn't listen to any more, and she could hardly see him for flashing lights. She said, 'I've got a migraine. I need to rest for a while.' She dragged herself up the staircase. She thought her father went on shouting after her, but she kept going until she could shut and lock the door of her bedroom, kick off her shoes and fall face down on the bed.

The pillow was cool against her face and she kept very still, trying to think. This was the main reason her father was determined to keep her and Martin apart. All that talk about Mr Jackson confiding in her father that Martin was worrying him to death. Her father had never had time to spare for anyone else's troubles. He was the great artist, completely self-centred. Nobody would come to him with their problems.

But when Martin said he had unfinished business here, could he have meant that 'sizeable amount of money' and a business deal that was not straight dealing? The Allens owed him, in a way. Maybe he was exacting some sort of payment. No, she thought. Martin would never deliberately go out of his way to hurt me because of what my father did. No, he likes me. He finds me attractive and he enjoyed being with me. Though Mrs Pomeroy was right, Martin Jackson was never going to learn to love an Allen.

But love wasn't in this. Nobody had said anything about love. Until last night. 'I love you,' she had said, and this morning Martin had gone. That little word had brought down the shutters, even though it was only a word and didn't mean anything.

Only it was true, and it meant everything. She loved him so much that there would never be anyone else and she would be lonely for ever. Pain racked her head and heart and she wept, tearless tearing sobs into the pillow. There was nothing ahead but a black void of endless days and nights, and nothing to remember, except everything he had done and said since he came back to Chadsford.

Why hadn't she let him make love to her last night? Why had Anton left that damnable home-made wine behind? Where was her pride? Martin had gone because Sandra had phoned him, and Lacey imagined them going to the cottage tonight and was seized with such murderous jealousy that she could almost believe it could transport her to arrive there in spirit. She would sit on the rocks and scream his name like Jet howling at the shapes in the moonlight. She couldn't bear the thought of Martin with somebody else, and she was going to make herself physically ill if she carried on like this. 'Glad nobody's getting hurt,' Mrs Pomeroy had just said, and Lacey thought, How much pain do you want? A very little more would kill me.

She struggled up to take some codeine, then lay down again and tried to think of nothing, because thoughts turned like knives in her brain. And at last she fell asleep.

She woke to a phone ringing, and didn't move a muscle until it stopped. The headache had subsided again. When she sat up slowly she found that she had slept for nearly three hours and that seemed to have settled her hangover. The heartache could be held down. It would have to be. Martin would have left by now, and she must get up and go down to the Centre, and brazen things out, because she would be living in this town for a long time.

She worked on her appearance, and with a change of clothing and her hair brushed on the surface—her scalp was tender—she could face herself in the mirror and decide, Not a bad job, if I do say so myself.

She swallowed another headache pill and escaped from the house without looking or listening for her father. Inside she felt like bleak winter, but the sun was still shining and the streets were busy, and she walked with a light step and smiled at the people she knew, hurrying on.

She was grabbed as soon as she reached the Centre, and this was where she had to stop, she was cornered now: 'Did you get locked in here last night?' was the first question put to her, and she grinned,

'Yes, we did, and I don't recommend it!' She ran up the staircase, and there was a whoop as she appeared at the head of the stairs. All her colleagues were waiting for her, and she dodged between the customers towards her own stall and Maisie and Porteus. 'What's all this, then?' Porteus boomed as she approached, and she said,

'I hadn't got my keys, that's what. And you locked the front door and the office.' Everybody was grinning, even the tourists were wondering what the joke was, and Lacey perched herself on her stool and said, 'Oh, very funny. You should all try it some time. It would be the death of you,' and she jerked her head towards Porteus. 'Do you know what we had to eat?' She reeled off what they had found, shuddering as her stomach lurched at the memory of crisps and chutney and damson wine.

'Anton's cousin's home-made wine was dynamite,' she said, and Maisie clucked sympathetically,

'Yes, you do look a bit ragged. How's Martin?'

'He stuck to Coke.' Lacey chuckled here, then told them, 'He had to go back to London this morning, but he'll try to come down again on Saturday.' She hoped it sounded casual and cheerful, and she went on about Jet howling at the shadows and maybe the place was haunted, and then she explained that while she had had a captive customer, so to speak, she'd sold quite a lot for them.

Martin would pay up, she knew, and he would have to collect some time. Until he did she would buy the things he'd ordered and he could knock it off what her father had owed his. She said none of that, of course, and suddenly Porteus rumbled, 'What about *Sweet Alice?*'

'Sorry, my old darling,' said Lacey blithely, 'but you're back in the cast. Somebody had better take in Martin's picture. We don't want to get done for false pretences.'

Paul turned up at lunchtime, and Lacey was thankful she was busy with a customer and could shake her head and say, 'I can't get away.' Paul hovered, but he would have preferred to talk to Lacey without an audience, and after a couple of minutes he said, 'I'll be back at six.' That delayed that scene, but it was inevitable sooner or later.

She knew it was going round town that Martin Jackson and Lacey Allen had got themselves locked in the Centre all night. It was a joke. The real news was that Martin had left town this morning when everybody had thought he was staying over the weekend. He could have been recalled, of course, but it seemed awfully sudden, and most of them decided that they would be surprised if he turned up again this side of next year's festival.

There was no dodging Denice. She came into the Centre during the afternoon smiling broadly, and she wouldn't have cared if Lacey had had a crowd of customers, she was having her say. Lacey could hardly blame her. Denice had spent a lot of time in the old days crying on Lacey's shoulder because Martin Jackson was keeping his distance. Lacey had comforted Denice and sometimes lost patience, but always shown her own dislike and distrust of Martin. And now they were saying that Lacey had had an affair with him while he lived here, and ever since he came back something had obviously been going on between them.

Denice didn't bother to keep the gleam out of her eyes, although she did stop smiling and adopt a mournful expression when she said, 'Poor Lacey, you do look rotten. I know how you're feeling.'

'Have you been on the damson wine too?' quipped Lacey flippantly, and Denice said softly,

'Don't be silly. I mean he's gone, hasn't he? Even sooner than you thought.'

Lacey straightened a print on the wall and Denice stood close beside her, almost whispering as though they were sharing secrets. 'You're lucky you've still got Paul,' she hissed. 'Seeing Martin again has made me realise I've a lot to be thankful for in Barry. They're the rocks.'

Lacey wanted to laugh. Compared with Martin, Paul and Barry were insignificant. Rocks? They were more like pebbles. 'You know where you are with them,' Denice went on earnestly. 'You take my advice—you get a hold on Paul.'

'You mean attach myself to the rock? Like a barnacle?' Lacey's lips curved and she managed to laugh a little. 'I think I'd rather hitch my wagon to a star. Give me a touch of danger any day.' She was babbling, acting like mad to hide her abysmal misery, and Denice said tartly,

'But you didn't get a chance to hitch your wagon, did you? He's gone.'

'You have a point there,' said Lacey.

If she had burst into tears Denice might have felt sorry for her. Maisie certainly would, but she would do her crying alone. Nobody would ever know for sure how it was for her.

Paul was waiting at five to six. She went downstairs and he was standing by the front door. When he saw her coming down he stepped into the office and as she reached the office door he said, 'I've got to talk to you.'

She had to go into the room. She couldn't conduct this conversation from the corridor, but she said, 'No, you haven't,' as she came closer to him.

'Do you know what they're saying?' Paul demanded.

'Yes,' she said. 'Yes, I do.'

'Is it true?' What Paul had been told in the last few hours had appalled him.

'Five years ago or last night?' Lacey said wearily. She blamed herself for the hurt in Paul's face, but she was so deeply hurt herself that the only way she could bear it was by refusing to feel anything. She said, 'Look, I'm sorry, but I'm beginning to wonder if I'm one of the fairground sideshows. I just wish everybody would shut up about Martin Jackson and leave me alone.'

'He's gone?' asked Paul.

'Yes.'

'But he's coming back on Saturday?'

She doubted that. Or perhaps he would come with Sandra. She shrugged, 'I wouldn't know,' and got a tirade of reproaches. Paul was washing his hands of her. He had his position to think of. Lacey had made a fool of herself, and he was convinced she was regretting it, but he was not having the assistants in the library sniggering behind his back.

A rock? she thought. It would be more like slipping into quicksands, eyes and ears stopped, everything muffled and stifled. She said, 'You've had a lucky escape. I'm not the girl you thought I was.' She couldn't say he was not the man she'd thought, because he was. She was the one who had wrecked the relationship.

She left him there and went back upstairs to tell Maisie that she would like to take up an earlier invitation and go round to their flat tonight for a snack meal with a few friends. This was how she would get through the days ahead, by filling them, and she managed the evening very well. It was typical of countless evenings. People she knew, food that could be eaten with fingers or forks—kebabs tonight—and somebody singing to a guitar.

Lacey joined in the songs, answered all the questions about Martin briefly and with a smile, and felt as if the small crowded room was empty. She wouldn't let herself think about him, not for a moment, until she was in her own bed, after midnight, when a picture of the cottage came into her mind, as vividly as if she was outside calling to him.

She went on calling, in her head, just his name, and then the pills blacked her out. She had never taken sleeping pills before. These were her father's. He had occasional bouts of insomnia. They meant that Lacey woke sluggish, but for these first few nights she wasn't risking dreams, or nightmares, or lying awake. She bathed her eyes in cold water and spattered it over her forehead before she was ready to face the world. If she hadn't set the alarm she probably wouldn't have woken, but this was her usual time, and she prepared her father's breakfast. There was no sign of him, and she was only slightly surprised and not particularly concerned to find him still in bed.

'Take it away,' he said, to the tray she was carrying.
She put it down on the chest of drawers and stood
looking at him, arms folded. Mrs Pomeroy had called
him a crafty old fox. Playing for sympathy now, Lacey
was sure, but she wasn't feeling sorry for him. She
wasn't asking how he had slept or how he was feeling.
She said, 'I'm off.'

'Jackson's gone, then?'

She turned to look back. 'By the way, how much was
it you owed his father?'

'Nothing,' said her father. 'I don't care what he told
you. The man's a liar.'

She nearly asked, 'Is Edith Pomeroy?' but she hadn't
the strength. As she left the house she looked at the
phone and thought. He won't ring and he won't come
back on Saturday. She felt hollow, numb. She could
hear herself talking and she did the things she had to
do, and none of it was real. It was as though she was
acting all the time.

Sweet Alice went on, with Porteus in his original part.
Of course he wasn't the star attraction Martin had
been, but nobody asked for their money back and
Lacey said her lines without faltering, and in the
dressing room they had stopped asking her questions
because she couldn't tell them anything. She didn't
know where Martin was. Working somewhere, she
thought, and yes, he had said he might come back on
Saturday. She gave no sign of pining. It was business as
usual. She even collected Jet and agreed with Mrs
Bowden that it was a shame Martin had had his leave
cut short.

There were no phone calls from him, not at the
Centre nor the house, and he had not rung anybody else
here either or the news would have been relayed to
Lacey. She didn't matter to him. Not now nor the last
time. He wouldn't have let Aunt Helena's small rebuff
put him off keeping in touch with her if it had really
mattered. The night of the storm had meant so much to

her and so little to him, and it could have been the same again. It was the same again. He was free of her, but she would never be free.

When the last performance of *Sweet Alice* finished on Friday afternoon Lacey breathed a sigh of heartfelt relief. Financially the production had been a fantastic success for the hospital, but emotionally, for Lacey, it had been a killer.

When she came out of the Little Theatre she walked up to the Pomeroys' house. She had phoned earlier and Mrs Pomeroy was out in the garden now, wearing a hat and thick gardening gloves, pruning off dead roses into a trug which was slung on her arm.

'I kept them going till the end of October last year,' she announced proudly as Lacey reached her. Lacey's bouquet of red roses was dwindling daily. She took them out reluctantly as the petals fell and from them there would be no second blooming.

'All right, are you?' Mrs Pomeroy peered into Lacey's face from under her flopping hat brim.

Lacey was flushed from the recent removal of the greasepaint and from the sun. She smiled and said yes, thank you, she was all right.

'Tea's waiting,' said Mrs Pomeroy. Lacey had checked that she would be in at four, but she hadn't wanted to stay for tea. She had only wanted to ask a question, and if Mrs Pomeroy was determined to be hospitable she hoped that tea would be poured in the kitchen.

No such luck. There was a tray with Spode china, cucumber sandwiches and a Victoria sponge, on a small highly polished table in the drawing room, and Mrs Pomeroy went off to the kitchen to bring in the silver teapot.

Lacey tried not to look at the sampler. She was still carrying the scars of that. And when she glanced down at the Chinese rug there was a faint stain beside the chair where she had sat drinking coffee with Martin on

Monday. She remembered kicking over the cup when she jumped to her feet, and wondered if she should apologise. She wondered how Martin had explained it. If he had taken the blame, or said it was Lacey, dashing out of the house like somebody going out of her mind.

'Milk or lemon?' asked Mrs Pomeroy.

'Er—milk, please.'

'And a slice of sponge?'

She didn't want anything. She had no appetite these days. There seemed no flavour in food. No colours, no scents. Everything was drab. But life had to go on, and that meant eating and talking sensibly and acting as though she was still alive.

She said, 'Thank you,' and Mrs Pomeroy cut a piece and lifted it on to a plate with a silver cake slice. 'I really didn't mean to put you to this trouble,' said Lacey. 'Cake and sandwiches and everything, I just wanted a few words.'

'I'm very relieved to see you looking so well,' said Mrs Pomeroy. 'I've got to admit I've had some anxious moments wondering if I'd spoken out of turn.'

Lacey smiled steadily, stirring her tea. 'He hasn't phoned you, has he?' asked Mrs Pomeroy, with what might have been hope, but when Lacey shook her head she said, 'I didn't think he would, and he hasn't phoned here either. He could be the other side of the world, of course. He's got a very interesting job.'

'Or he could still be on leave, and spending the last few days with Sandra,' said Lacey gaily. She had faced that so often that she could say it without choking, and Mrs Pomeroy, who thought that was exactly what was happening, sighed and asked, 'What did you want to see me about?'

'About what you told me,' said Lacey. 'My father won't discuss it. He said there was a business deal that fell through, and he won't tell me any more. He says there's nothing to discuss, but I would like to know how much was involved.'

Mrs Pomeroy and Aunt Helena had been lifelong friends. Her husband owned a law firm. She knew the full story. Around six years ago, Lacey thought, and that wasn't so very long ago. 'Oh no,' said Mrs Pomeroy.

'I want to pay it back,' said Lacey, which started Mrs Pomeroy so much that she forgot her determination to say no more and gasped,

'My dear child, I don't think you could raise that kind of money!'

So it *was* a sizeable sum, and Lacey's only capital was the Centre. She said, 'I might be able to mortgage the Centre, borrow on it,' and Mrs Pomeroy looked so distressed that she went on, 'Well, I was thinking about it.'

'You think about it,' said Mrs Pomeroy, meaning, 'You forget it,' and the talk switched, getting back to the festival which was proving such a success. Lacey should be proud that she was the one who had brought up the idea in the first place, said Mrs Pomeroy; and Lacey thought how ironic that was, and said yes, she supposed so, because it had brought in the trade, and benefited the charities, and really it had been a lot of fun....

Saturday would see the end of it. Things wouldn't really change after Saturday, Lacey would never be the same again, but at least the flags would come down and the music would stop, and the razzamatazz would be over. Everything would look normal again.

There was a final gala ball, the Runaway Mop Dance, being held in the town hall to wind up Festival Fortnight, and most of the locals had tickets. All the Centre folk and all Lacey's social circle. She should have been going with Paul, but she hadn't seen him since Tuesday and on Saturday morning Tessa, who had popped into the Centre after the library, told her that Paul didn't think he could make it. Tessa had asked if they'd be seeing him tonight and he had said he'd always considered dancing a waste of time.

Did this mean Lacey wasn't going? Tessa enquired. All of them were wondering if it was ever going to be Lacey-and-Paul again. 'Sure I'm going,' said Lacey. 'Martin hasn't come back, has he?' was Tessa's next question and Lacey had lost count of the number of times she had been asked that today already. He had said he would try for Saturday and like an idiot she had repeated what he'd said, and today was Saturday and they all seemed to be waiting. She said now what she kept on saying, 'If he has I haven't seen him.'

She would have heard the moment his car was spotted. He wasn't in town, but she would go to the dance tonight so that nobody wondered if she was sitting at home praying for the phone to ring. She could have told them the watched pot never boils and the watched phone never rings, and Martin would not be coming and he would not be phoning.

Her father might have attended the ball if he had not still been hoping to make her feel guilty. Since she had faced him with Mrs Pomeroy's accusation he had been playing the injured party, withdrawn and cut to the quick. He had not been neglected. Lacey had devoted herself less to his creature comforts, but she had arranged with someone who could use the extra cash to help with the cleaning and cooking. Laurence Allen hadn't commented on the fact that the woman who had looked after him last weekend while Lacey was in Eastbourne was still serving up the occasional meal. He expected Lacey's show of independence to crumble quite soon, but if he precipitated a scene she might flare up with some nonsense about moving out, even going away. He was fond of his daughter. He loved her as he had loved his sister, so far as it was in him to love anyone but himself.

'No,' he said, when Lacey asked on Saturday evening if he was attending the Runaway Mop Dance. He was sitting in the drawing room, listening to soft music, with a glass of port and an open book. Mrs Brown had fed him again. It was nearly seven o'clock and Lacey had been walking Jet since six and just taken him home to the wool shop. She opened the drawing room door, her hair looking windblown, her skin fresh and glowing from a three-mile hike over the hills.

'I have found the last two weeks,' said Laurence Allen, 'very taxing, not to say debilitating. I'm in no mood for a ball.'

'In that case,' she said briskly, 'may I have your ticket?'

He deduced she was not going with Paul Behague. He knew that Martin Jackson had left town but that he might be back today, and he couldn't stop himself asking 'Jackson back?' Lacey took the ticket from the drawer in a bureau and said, 'Not yet, but till midnight there's hope.'

She didn't know why she said that, except that she was angry with him, sitting there smug as a well-fed cat. She was ashamed of him who had always been her pride, because he was greedy as well as selfish. He had cheated Martin's father and left her saddled with debt as well as heartbreak. She went out of the drawing room up to her own room and put the ticket down on the dressing table.

She would pay back some of the debt. She would insist on it. She could borrow on the Centre, and if Martin wouldn't take it he could name another charity. He had done well for charity these last two weeks, what with the hiring mop and *Sweet Alice*. Oh, how she wished that tonight was over! Tonight and the next ten years.

She dressed with care. She would be noticed tonight—not just as Lacey Allen, who was a nice girl with nothing exceptional about her except that her father was a famous artist, but because her steady had dropped her like a hot coal, and Martin Jackson had come and gone and that was obviously the end of that. She covered her face with her hands and thought— Don't cry, don't cry. If your eyes are red somebody will see.

It was a sultry evening. She had a dress in white lawn with a full frill at the throat, sleeves with a narrow cuff at the wrists, and a full skirt. A wide crystal-studded sash cinched in the waist, or it could be worn flowing, and if the ballroom was too crowded or hot she could always take off her sash. If she felt like running free. Or just running, if it all got too much.

'Shall we come up for you?' Maisie had suggested when Lacey left the Centre at six, and Lacey had said, 'I'll meet you there at eight.' She knew she would be alone; and Maisie thought so too, and she and Porteus would stay by Lacey as long as she needed them, Lacey was grateful for that, but surely she could manage the ten-minute stroll down to the town hall on her own. She had to. She had to bluff her way through tonight, and then at least the festival would be over and she would know for sure that Martin was not coming back.

At eight o'clock the streets were empty, except for locals, and holidaymakers who were staying in the hotels. Lacey in her pretty white dress got some admiring glances, but they slid over her. When she passed Martin's old home she hesitated for a moment, looking at it from across the road. It didn't look very different from five years ago, but Martin was never going to walk out of that door again.

Porteus and Maisie were waiting for her. She was a few minutes late, but they were still in the crowded foyer near the door and Porteus spotted Lacey as she walked in. 'We've bagged a table,' said Maisie, and Lacey found herself, surrounded by her colleagues, being ushered up the great curved staircase into a seat in the ballroom, behind a floral arrangement where she could stay almost hidden for the rest of the evening if she chose.

In fact it wasn't too bad. She could get along fine in crowds. It was being alone she dreaded, because that was when she thought about the cottage and the island, and feelings flooded back in a surge of jealousy, and when that receded a terrible sensation of loss and bereavement. But here, with everyone smiling around her, she smiled too.

On the anniversary of the runaway mop the board from a fortnight ago was up on the side of the stage where the band was playing. Everyone who had 'hired' had paid up, and all services had been satisfactorily discharged. Lacey's name was called and she had to stand up and say 'Yes,' and the vicar had Martin's cheque. Four meals she was supposed to have supplied. She knew they would be wondering what and when, and before long they would be asking: brandy snaps, Denice's buffet, lunchtime sausages, and crisps and chutney. Everybody had a quick look-around while they were clapping, in case Martin reappeared unnoticed to take a bow with Lacey, which was highly improbable; and then the vicar went on the next name.

The catering was good. An adjoining room had a buffet table running round three walls, and a bar doing a brisk trade. Lacey put off eating, there was plenty and she wasn't hungry. She drank iced white wine, and danced with everyone who asked her, and chattered, and smiled when they enquired about Martin, 'He may be back, I don't know.'

Then she saw him walk into the ballroom and her heart stopped beating. She was partnering Anton, there was a mass of dancers between her and the door, but Martin saw her right away, and she said, 'Excuse me,' and began pushing her way towards him. She didn't care who saw, or what they thought, or even if Sandra was with him. She was usually a considerate girl, but she shoved now, and a few of the dancers looked huffy and surprised.

All right, there was no future in it, but he had the

power to draw her to him, and wherever she was if he walked into a room she would go to meet him. 'Well,' she said, as she reached him, 'you made it!' She was alive again. The world was bright and beautiful.

'Coming?' he asked.

'Why not?' She didn't pretend to consider, and they walked out of the ballroom, down the curving staircase, through the foyer and the big open door on to the pavement. They were watched every step of the way. Martin had been recognised as soon as he came in, and almost everyone here tonight knew Lacey. If they had hesitated for a moment somebody would have stopped them, if it was only to say 'Hello' to Martin. But they went fast, just getting out, leaving a buzz of voices and a sea of startled faces.

Outside they went on walking, taking the first side street off the main road. Then he asked, 'How's the hangover?'

'Much better, thank you.' There were fewer people here. A few shops, with lighted windows but doors closed, then a terrace of houses. They walked side by side, not hand-holding, and Lacey asked, 'What's been happening to you since Tuesday morning?'

'This and that.'

'I'll bet.' Even if it was Sandra and the cottage he was here now, and she was not quite so jealous, and she could almost sound amused.

'Is Paul at the dance?'

'Paul doesn't care for dancing.'

'Shall we walk?' he said. They were coming to a path on to the hills, and she said gravely, 'Let's. It was hot in there.'

It was warm out here, but not like that other night when storm had been threatening all day. The hot spell would probably break before long; tomorrow night perhaps, or the next, but tonight was just still and warm with a clear starry sky overhead.

But they walked as they had that other night, and she

thought, just being with you is companionship, even if neither of us says a word. We'll go back to the charcoal burner's hut, she thought. It's a ruin, but who needs a roof on a night like this? and it won't change his life, but it won't be the end because we shall meet again, And again, I'll see to that.

She wasn't dressed for striding through the heather, her skirt was too long. She lifted it in both hands and said, 'I seem to have trouble with petticoats.'

'Pretty dress,' said Martin. They followed a track and then walked on soft turf over the hills, and Lacey asked quietly, 'Was it a lot of money?'

'What?' He stopped and looked at her. 'Who told you?' he said. 'Not your old man?'

'Mrs Pomeroy, but she wouldn't say how much, and I want to pay it back.'

Martin chuckled, 'I'll bet your old man doesn't.'

'No,' Lacey had to admit. 'Was it that art gallery or what? I'd like to hear all about it.'

'No, you wouldn't,' and he took her hand to walk on, but she held back.

'Mrs Pomeroy said my father swindled your father.'

'Not the right word for the wife of a lawyer to be using,' said Martin. He was smiling, white teeth against the tan of his skin.

'He died poor. Everybody was surprised. Aren't you bitter about that?'

'Good lord, no.' He didn't sound bitter. 'He had a life income, he'd always have known where his next meal was coming from, and he never did a real day's work in his life. Your father outsmarted him, which wasn't hard. So did fifty others, although it was Laurence Allen who hit the jackpot.'

He was talking with affectionate tolerance. Lacey remembered his father, a handsome, distinguished man. Martin had never known his mother, there had only been his father, and she asked, 'How did you get on with him?'

'Fine,' said Martin. 'In some ways he was like your father—king of his own little world, selfish as hell. I always knew I was on my jack. It didn't bother me.'

He had always had the strength of the born winner and the charisma to attract others. A leader and a loner, and Lacey had been a lonely child, reared in a house from which there was no escape and in which she was allowed no growth. 'Did Aunt Helena know about the money?' she asked.

'I presume so.' If Edith Pomeroy did, Aunt Helena would, and she could have opened that first letter in error, they were both Miss Allen. 'I suppose,' mused Lacey, 'that would be another reason why she didn't want you and me getting friendly. You did write?' He looked at her and she asked, 'Do you remember what you said?'

They sat down. The hill, rising behind them, hid the lights of the town. Ahead the moors stretched away. Martin said, 'I asked you to come to Cambridge for the weekend so that we could talk, I could take you around and you could meet my friends. When I got no answer I wrote again and said I'd ring and when.'

His voice was quiet and flat and Lacey thought, Well, he tried, but not too hard; and she remembered the agony of waiting—but Martin wouldn't understand that. 'And Aunt Helena answered,' she said. 'Why didn't you ring again?'

'Why didn't you ring at all?' His voice was suddenly quicker, rougher. 'You could have got my phone number or address from any number of folk.'

'I was scared,' she admitted.

'What do you think I was?'

'Scared? You?'

'Yes. That night when I walked out of the old house I was on my own. I always had been. I never thought I needed anybody. But when I saw you coming towards me I wasn't even surprised. I just felt that we two together was how it should be. The next day I was scared I'd blown it. I wasn't even too clear how it had happened, whether it was rape or seduction or who took who, but in the cold light I thought you might decide you could do without a character who didn't even stop to say by-your-leave. You had a comfortable home and a civilised life, I couldn't blame you for not wanting a wild man disrupting it.'

There was something primitive about the sheer animal beauty of him, in his power and strength. But there was a tenderness and a caring and she had gloried in their lovemaking, 'Mind you,' he added, 'for a long time I hoped you'd get in touch.'

'You never came back,' she said.

'Not until I thought I could meet you and feel nothing, but the moment I looked at you it was as though it had only been a few days, I was right back. I couldn't believe it. I couldn't stand letting you out of my sight. When you wouldn't come to that Country and Western session I stood outside your house waiting for you to come out with the dog!'

She had gone through the back gate, down to the pub to catch him. 'I walked him with Sandra on Sunday,' Martin went on. 'Over the hills here, and all the time I was missing you.'

She had been in Eastbourne, thinking of him, and soon she would tell him. But now she sat and listened and hoped with all her heart that this was true. 'I realised,' he said, smiling so perhaps he wasn't all that serious, 'that I've never fallen for a girl who didn't have something of you in her. There's never been one with straight hair. Once I was turned on by a girl with laryngitis because of her husky voice.' Now he had to be joking, although Sandra had curly hair. 'But you're the only one who's ever driven me wild,' he told her. 'Except with you I have the reputation of being a cool customer.'

He was cool now, she thought, sitting beside her, maybe weighing his words. She wanted him to take her in his arms. For him she was wild with wanting. 'Did you go the cottage on Tuesday?' she asked. She shouldn't be asking, making him think of anywhere but here.

'Yes.'

'With Sandra?' Or think of anyone but her. This was *stupid*.

'I always go there alone,' he said. 'It's my bolt-hole.'

'Why did you go?' She ran her fingers over the soft springy grass.

'You might not remember,' he said, 'But just before you flaked out you said, "I love you".'

'I did?'

'I knew it was the damson wine talking, but I was stone sober and when you said that I wanted to shout it and hold you and never let you go; and I thought I'd better get away and do some thinking, because when I can reach out and touch you I seem to lose all logic.

'So I went to the cottage. I thought, if I can do without her I'll come back, I'll see Paul off, and she's coming round to me. We'll get there eventually because I am the one for her, and she half knows it even if she isn't convinced. I won't go rushing things this time and grabbing the girl. I'll give her all the time she needs. Only please God it won't be another five years.'

His profile was hard and haggard in the moonlight, 'There was no beauty there without you,' he said. 'That's how it is with me, there's nothing worth having anywhere unless you're sharing it.' He reached blindly for her hand, 'I want you to marry me,' he said. 'I think I've always been married to you and I know I always will be.' He cupped her face, looking down into it, and she felt his fingers trembling. So did his voice. 'Oh, Lacey, I can't—I can't find the words to tell you how much I love you.'

There was music in the air, the fair was playing itself

out; and the grass was soft beneath them as she linked her tightening arms around his neck, 'Then show me,' she said.

Get this book FREE!